GO WELL, STAY WELL

Go Well, Stay Well

TOECKEY JONES

HARPER & ROW, PUBLISHERS

NEW YORK

Cambridge
Hagerstown
Philadelphia
San Francisco

London
Mexico City
São Paulo
Sydney

1817

Library of Congress Cataloging in Publication Data
Jones, Toeckey.
    Go well, stay well.

    SUMMARY: A white girl in South Africa finds out
how difficult it is to be friends with a black girl.
    [1. Friendship—Fiction.   2. Race relations—
Fiction.   3. South Africa—Race relations—Fiction]
I. Title.
PZ7. J7275Go 1980   [Fic]   79-3603
ISBN 0-06-023061-4
ISBN 0-06-023062-2 lib. bdg.

For my mother and Chris,
and in memory of Jim Manabile

I

'Damn!' Candy swore softly.

Her sandal strap had snapped. It was the final straw.

Everything, but everything, had gone wrong that morning. She had woken up with a headache; Colin had been in one of his worst big-brother, know-it-all moods at breakfast; she had run for the bus, only to see it move off just before she reached the terminus. Then she had had to wait twenty minutes for the next; and when she had finally got to town she had found it busier than usual, the department stores crowded with impatient shoppers, making it impossible even to see the display counters, let alone get anywhere near them to choose a birthday present for her father.

And now, dodging parcels, prams, pushcarts and elbows as she hurried along the pavement towards a tobacconist's to get cigars as a last resort, her sandal had to go and give up on her. It was enough to make her want to give up, herself, and go straight home.

But she couldn't do that. Her father's birthday was on Tuesday; she had to get him something, there wouldn't be another opportunity. Dragging her left foot, with the loose sandal strap flapping, she went on as best she could.

And then, inevitably it seemed, with her stars so obviously criss-crossed against her, somebody stepped on the trailing strap, instantly tripping her up. It happened so fast there was no time to try and break her fall. The next thing she knew, she was lying full length on the cool, dusty pavement, with legs, seemingly hundreds of legs, flashing past her. In sudden panic that she would be crushed, she scrambled awkwardly to her feet, vaguely aware of hands helping her.

'Are you all right, dear?'

7

'Yes, thank you, I'm fine,' she muttered. 'I'm fine . . . thank you,' and she stepped back hurriedly into the mainstream of pedestrians, driven by her need to escape being the centre of focus among so many strangers.

However, she hadn't gone more than a few paces when the fierce pain in her left leg forced her to stop. Looking down, she saw her ankle was swollen, the puffy area around the joint already turning blue. Suddenly feeling faint, she closed her eyes.

Next moment a passerby knocked her shoulder, sending her weight on to her left leg so that she cried out in agony. But it also brought her to her senses; she had to get out of the crowd before further damage was done. Nobody was now interested in her predicament; standing still she had become an obstacle to the general flow of people. Gritting her teeth, she hobbled sideways to the edge of the pavement where she leaned against a lamp-post, closing her eyes and waiting for the worst of the pain to ease before thinking what to do next.

Almost immediately she felt a tentative touch on her arm. She opened her eyes to see a young African girl standing directly in front of her, her face almost level with her own. Instinctively, Candy's grip on her bag tightened. The girl could be after her money. Candy knew how nimble-fingered the young black pickpockets in the city were reputed to be; she was forever being warned to keep a close hold on her purse.

'You okay?' Without waiting for an answer, the girl bent down to inspect Candy's ankle. 'Tch . . . tch . . . shame.' Shaking her head sorrowfully, she straightened up. 'That's no good to walk on,' she decided.

'It'll be all right. I'll sit down for a few minutes, then I'll be okay.' Candy smiled thinly, her eyes still warily watching the girl's every move.

Shyly, the girl grinned back. 'You can sit down in the park,' she said. 'It's not too far.'

8

'Yes, I'll do that. I'll be all right now . . . thank you.'

Just then somebody bumped the girl's shoulder, causing her to stagger forward closer to Candy. 'Too many people,' she said, her grin broadening to show sparkling white teeth.

'Yes.' Candy's fingers had tightened even more firmly round her bag. Bracing herself, she put a little weight on her left leg and then grimaced as pain flared through her ankle.

'Come, I must help you.' Hesitantly, the girl took hold of Candy's free arm, and after a momentary reluctance, Candy cautiously allowed herself to be supported as they began to move slowly along the gutter.

'Too many drinks, hey?' the girl teased.

Candy managed a laugh, then felt herself blushing as she became aware of the curious stares they were attracting. She tried to hobble faster, leaning as little as possible on the supporting arm beside her. She still wasn't sure she could trust the girl; and anyway, she didn't like being under an obligation to her. It would have been so much simpler if it had been a white person who had offered help. She didn't know why the girl was doing it. Should she offer to pay her? It was all rather embarrassing.

The park was only two blocks away, but it seemed an age before they got there. As the girl helped her down into a sitting position on the grass, Candy was aware of her bag slipping off her shoulder and the girl stretching out to catch it as it fell. Candy held her breath, her heart racing. But the girl didn't run off. Instead, she waited until Candy was sitting comfortably, and then handed the bag down to her.

'Better now?' she asked.

Candy could only nod, feeling ashamed.

The girl turned away and crouched down to take a closer look at the injured ankle. While she explored the swelling with careful, gentle fingers, Candy studied her thoughtfully.

She was really rather pretty, Candy discovered somewhat to her surprise, for she had never thought of African features as being particularly attractive before. But this girl's features were all in perfect proportion to each other, giving her face as a whole an open, sunny expression.

The girl looked up and caught Candy staring at her. Grinning foolishly, Candy asked, 'Well, do you think I'll live?'

The girl also grinned. 'For sure, I can't say. Maybe.'

She had very large, deep brown, glowing eyes. Full of mischief, Candy thought.

But an instant later the eyes had darkened into seriousness. 'Is it very sore?' the girl asked, scrunching up her face as if she was in pain herself.

'No, it's much better now. Thanks so much for all your help. I don't know what I would have done without it.'

'It's nothing.' The girl stood up shrugging, and smoothed down her faded, floral-patterned skirt which Candy noticed had a large patch near the hem.

It occurred to Candy that the girl might think she was trying to get rid of her, not needing her help any more. But Candy didn't want her to go. She had never met an African girl of her own age before – at least not to speak to. And she was already beginning to like the slender, gawky figure in front of her who seemed undecided about her next move and was fidgeting nervously with the frayed collar of her blouse, trying to do up a button that wasn't there.

'Are you in a hurry?' Candy asked.

'No. Why? Can I give you a lift home? My Mercedes is just round the corner.'

Candy laughed and that apparently decided the girl. She flopped suddenly, all limbs and awkward angles like a puppy, on to the grass beside Candy.

'What's your name?' she asked.

'Candice. But everyone calls me Candy. And yours?'

'Rebecca. But everyone calls me Becky.' And then they both laughed.

'Tell you what,' Candy said. 'I'm thirsty. How about you?'

'Sure. What would you like? I'll go and get it. Whisky? Beer?'

'In my condition I think I'd better stick to Coke. But let's go and sit down somewhere and maybe have something to eat as well. So long as I don't have to walk too far my ankle should be all right.'

'You know a place we can go?' Becky asked.

Candy's face slowly reddened into acute embarrassment. For a moment she had completely forgotten. There wasn't anywhere they could go together. Within ten minutes' walk of where they were sitting there were at least three restaurants or coffee bars. But Becky couldn't go into them; they were all exclusively for whites. Further away there were a few cafés inadequately catering for the African workers travelling daily into Johannesburg from the black township of Soweto. But even if Candy could have walked that far with her bad ankle, she would be stopped from entering any of them with Becky.

'Do you want us to get arrested?' Becky teased.

Candy tried to smile, but she felt more angry than amused. After looking at her for a moment, Becky stopped laughing and dug into the voluminous pocket of her skirt.

'Here,' she said. 'We can eat this.' She held out a small Easter egg.

Candy shook her head. She couldn't take Becky's chocolate. The egg was hardly big enough for two. Besides, Becky looked as though she could do with a few square meals, let alone one meagre mouthful of chocolate.

'It's spare. It's the truth. I came into town to get Easter eggs for my small cousins, and I got this one to have on the train going home. We might as well share it now. Look, it's melting already.'

'No, honestly, I'm thirsty more than hungry. You have it.'

'Okay.' Becky tore the wrapping off the egg and popped

it into her mouth, licking her fingers with noisy enjoyment after she had finished chewing.

'Isn't it rather early to be buying Easter eggs?' Candy asked. 'Easter is still weeks away.'

'So?' Becky grinned. 'Hey! You want me to go and get you a Coke? There's a kiosk not too far.' She pointed vaguely across the park.

'Can you get us something to eat as well?'

'They sell sandwiches.'

'That'll do fine.' Candy was on the point of opening her bag when she remembered that she didn't have any change, only a five rand note. She was reluctant to produce it, not because she was any longer afraid that Becky might run off with it, but because she was embarrassed at revealing how much money she carried with her as a matter of course. To her, five rand represented only one week's pocket money; to Becky it might well seem a small fortune. However, Becky was hovering expectantly, so she had no option but to hand the note up to her.

'I'll run fast as a rabbit,' Becky promised.

She was back within a few minutes. Crouching down beside Candy, she carefully counted out the change aloud, before passing it across.

'All there,' she said soberly, but her eyes seemed to be laughing at Candy.

Candy put the money into her purse without looking at it, and busied herself opening the packets of sandwiches. She was sure Becky must have sensed her earlier mistrust and was now teasing her about it.

After a moment, she said a little stiffly, 'Which do you like more? Ham or egg?'

'I don't mind. I eat anything.' Becky stared doggedly until Candy had to look at her. As soon as she did, Becky broke into a wide, warm smile. Candy found herself smiling back, and suddenly they were both laughing.

'Here,' Candy said. 'You have the ham then. I prefer egg.' She suspected Becky didn't get a chance to eat ham very often. 'Cheers.' She held up her can of Coke. 'Here's to us.'

'Cheers,' Becky repeated, also raising her cold drink. 'To us and to our Prime Minister.'

'What on earth for?'

'For allowing us to sit together in the sunshine in this park. A few years ago we couldn't have, and then we wouldn't have become friends.'

Candy felt that in a roundabout way she was being put to some kind of test. 'I'll drink to *that*,' she said, 'but not to our Prime Minister.'

Becky nodded, apparently satisfied, and started tucking into her sandwich.

'Why aren't you eating?' she asked shortly.

'I'm really not very hungry.'

'I'm always hungry. My uncle says I must have a tape worm, but I tell him I just want to grow up big and strong like him. He likes that; it makes him feel, you know, like I'm his daughter. He doesn't have any daughters, you see, just three boys. "Boys," he always says, "too much trouble, boys." ' She giggled fondly.

'Tell me about your family,' Candy said.

In between bites at a second sandwich, Becky told her about her uncle (he was a very good man, she said) who ran a general store in Soweto; about her mother, who together with her aunt, helped him in the store; about a second uncle and aunt who lived with them; and finally she talked about her three boy cousins: Luke, aged eleven – four years younger than Becky, and Moses and Jeremiah, aged seven and five respectively. Apparently they all lived together in the one house.

'I hope it's a large house,' Candy said.

For some reason, Becky found that very funny.

'How many rooms are there?' Candy asked.

13

'Four. There's two bedrooms, a living-room and a kitchen.'

'Is that *all*?'

Becky nodded. 'There's no bathroom. The lavatory is outside in the yard . . . We wash in the kitchen,' she added, anticipating Candy's next question.

'Good God! Only four rooms. Where on earth do you all sleep?'

'My "big" uncle and aunt sleep in one bedroom, my "little" uncle and aunt sleep in the other, and my mother, myself and my three cousins all sleep in the living-room.'

'*All* of you in the one room? Is it very big?'

'Not too big,' Becky said, obviously enjoying Candy's increasingly horrified reactions. 'Maybe from here to that bench there, and then across to the path. Maybe a bit smaller than that.'

Candy stared at the area she had indicated. It was no more than ten feet long by thirteen feet, at the most, wide. She tried to imagine five people lying down in it.

'We don't sleep on beds,' Becky explained. 'We sleep on mats and roll them up in the morning, so there's space for everyone to sit during the day if we're all at home.' She shrugged. 'We all fit in okay really. We're lucky. In lots of houses, seven, eight or more people have to share one room. All the houses are small, you know.'

'Yes?' Candy couldn't help blushing at her exposed ignorance. She had known that housing in Soweto was inadequate, but she had had no idea what it was really like to live there. It all seemed so unreal, so far removed from her own experience, that it was barely conceivable. But she didn't doubt that Becky was telling her the truth. And discomforting as it was, now that she had the opportunity to find out all the facts, she knew she had to.

'What about electricity?' she asked.

Becky nodded. 'We're lucky. Too many houses don't. We're lucky to have water inside too. Lots of houses only have a tap in the yard. But there are no lights in the street. Very few streets are properly lit in Soweto. That's why we don't go out at night; we're too frightened. There are plenty of *tsotsis** everywhere.'

'I can imagine,' Candy said sympathetically. The violence in the township was something she had known about. She remembered reading somewhere that Soweto's crime rate was one of the highest in the world. Or was it the highest? She couldn't quite remember.

She wanted to ask Becky about her father, but she didn't like to in case Becky was intentionally not mentioning him for some reason. Perhaps he had died recently – been murdered even – and the memory was still painful.

Instead, Candy said, 'You don't have any brothers or sisters then?'

'I don't know. I might have.'

'Oh . . . What do you mean?'

'I'm my mother's only child, but I don't know about my father. He didn't marry my mother and he left her before I was born. Maybe he has lots of other children by now.'

'You've never met him?'

'No. I know his name, that's all. My mother doesn't even know where he is. He just went . . . disappeared.' Becky clicked her fingers dramatically like a magician.

'Oh . . .' Candy struggled to hide her embarrassment. She had been brought up to believe that illegitimacy was something shameful. But Becky didn't look at all ashamed, which made any expression of sympathy seem out of place. Suddenly, she appeared to Candy to be a lot older than herself, although Candy knew that they were the same age.

'What about your family?' Becky asked.

'What about them?' After everything Becky had told her, Candy was decidedly reluctant to talk about her own background.

* *thugs*

15

'Have you got any brothers or sisters?'

'I've got a brother.'

'Older or younger?'

'He's eighteen – three years older than me.'

'Mhhm! Is he nice?'

Candy wriggled uncomfortably. Becky's eyes were impishly bright, watching her to see how she reacted to the implied suggestion.

'He's got pimples . . . And he's conceited.' She was telling the truth, but she realized immediately afterwards that Becky might think she was trying to put her off. To sound more convincing Candy was about to add, 'I wouldn't wish him on my worst enemy,' when an ingrained sense of family loyalty stopped her.

'Too bad,' Becky said cheerfully. 'Hey, you still haven't eaten your sandwiches.'

'The Coke's made me full. You have them.' Candy held out the packet, but Becky was leaning forward to inspect the injured ankle.

'How's it feeling now?' she asked.

'Fine. Very much better, it really is.'

'You know, I might have to take you back to Soweto with me.'

'Why?'

Becky pointed to the ankle. 'Looks like you're turning black.' As Candy laughed, she went on, 'I can tell you, what you need is some castor oil.'

'You must be crazy.'

'It's the truth. Castor oil makes anything better – bruises, broken bones, belly-ache, bad temper.'

'Oh, come on now.'

Becky shrugged, smiling. 'My grandmother used to think so. She used to make me take it nearly every day. . . . "Haai! Haai! Haai! you sneezing child?" she used to say. "You got the devil inside you, that's the troubles. Au! we'll fix him" –

16

and she'd go to get her Holy Spirit in the bottle, as she called it. That's when I learned to run fast like a rabbit.'

'In more ways than one, I'll bet.'

But either Becky wasn't listening or she hadn't understood what Candy meant, because her expression immediately sobered. 'How are you going to get home?' she asked.

'I'll have to ring my dad and ask him to come and fetch me,' Candy told her, adding with a smile, 'He doesn't have a Mercedes though.'

'Tch! . . . tch! . . . Too bad. Hey, if you like, I can help you to the phone. There's one near the kiosk.'

'You might as well finish these off first. There's no hurry.'

Candy handed Becky the sandwiches and lay back in the sunshine. She was enjoying Becky's company too much to want to hasten their parting. Besides, her parents were likely to be in the middle of lunch right then; it was better to wait until they had finished before phoning. Candy imagined her father would be irritable at having to come and fetch her, although he would no doubt do his best not to show it. She remembered him saying at breakfast that he wanted to spend the whole day in the garden without interruption. He had been cross because Stephen had put compost in all the wrong places during the week, and he was convinced that some of his more delicate plants would suffer as a result.

Stephen was a middle-aged African who had been helping her father in the garden ever since Candy could remember. Her father employed him to do all the necessary, unskilled jobs that take up so much time in any large garden, and he came to their house every Monday, Wednesday and Thursday.

It suddenly occurred to Candy that she knew nothing whatsoever about Stephen. Apart from replying to his respectful greeting when he arrived in the morning, she had never actually spoken to him. His familiar figure housed a complete stranger because she had never shown any interest in

17

him. All he meant to her was a shabby, almost faceless form she was used to seeing moving about the garden with slow, lumbering steps, and who came and went regularly week after week.

She turned to look at Becky who was happily chewing her way through the last sandwich.

'Want a bite before it's too late?' Becky asked.

Not wanting Becky to think she might be reluctant to share a sandwich Becky had already bitten into, Candy immediately said, 'Okay. But only a small one,' and opened her mouth, intending Becky to hold the sandwich up to her.

However, Becky, obviously believing that Candy would prefer to break off a bit herself, was trying to thrust the sandwich into her hand. There was some embarrassed fumbling before Candy took a desperate bite at the bread, almost biting Becky's finger at the same time. They ended up laughing, with the result that Candy choked on her mouthful, and Becky had to scramble to her feet and pummel her on the back.

'I suppose I'd better go and make that phone call now,' Candy said reluctantly when she had recovered enough to speak.

Becky, standing at her side, immediately clasped her hands and bowed. 'Let me help you, Missus,' she offered.

Candy dragged herself hurriedly upright, ignoring the hand Becky held out to her. She didn't believe Becky was mocking her personally, but she didn't find her act at all funny. The last thing Candy wanted right then was to have their opposite positions in society forced into focus, even as a joke.

It didn't help that her ankle had now started to throb violently, having been jolted in her haste to get up unaided. Candy tried to take her weight off it, balancing precariously on one leg. She was in danger of toppling over when she felt Becky grasp her arm lightly to steady her.

'Thanks,' Candy said curtly.

Becky's fingers closed more firmly round her elbow, and they began to move slowly along the path. They hadn't gone more than a few paces when Candy started to regret the way she had reacted. The silence between them was the tense, uncomfortable silence of strangers. Candy felt she ought to say something, but she didn't know what.

'Okay?' Becky asked in a polite, distant tone.

'Yes, thanks.' Remorsefully, Candy added, 'I really don't know what I would have done without you.' She looked at Becky apologetically.

Becky shrugged. 'It's nothing.' Suddenly she stopped and began to giggle. 'You know, you look just like an old woman. We'll have to get you a wheelchair.'

The way she said 'we' made Candy feel that everything was all right again between them. And as they continued at a leisurely pace, she found she no longer gave a damn about people staring at them.

After Candy had made her phone call, they bought two more cold drinks, and then Becky helped her back to the park.

'I'm in no hurry,' Becky assured her. 'It's a good chance to improve my suntan.' She lay back on the grass, holding up her arm as if to admire the tan she already had.

'You're lucky you don't go red and burn like I do,' Candy told her.

'Sshh!' Becky warned. 'Nobody is allowed to be red in this country.'

A group of black youths passing nearby turned at the sound of their laughter. One of them narrowed his eyes and scrutinized Candy slowly, before calling out something to Becky in an African language. Whatever he said caused his companions to start sniggering. Looking angry, Becky shouted a short reply, at which the whole group burst into noisy guffaws.

19

'Stupid *tsotsis*,' Becky muttered as the youths slouched off.

'What did he say?' Candy asked. The way in which the youth had stared at her had made her feel intensely uncomfortable, and also a little nervous.

Becky shook her head. 'Damn *tsotsis*.'

'But what did he say?'

'It doesn't matter.'

'I'd like to know. He said something about me, didn't he?'

'Okay.' Becky broke into a half-grin. 'If you must know, he said you were . . . you know . . . sexy. He told me to get your telephone number for him.'

'Really?'

Candy couldn't help feeling shocked. Black men were not supposed to look at white women like that. The law forbade sexual relations across the Colour Bar, and such unions were not only illegal, they were also commonly considered to be indecent, if not an actual religious sin. The possibility of any sort of relationship developing between herself and a black boy had therefore never occurred to Candy. Nor had she ever, even briefly, wondered whether she found black men attractive. The only black men she had come across were servants in white households, and their servility had stamped them with an almost sexless identity in her mind.

She remembered the challenging arrogance in the youth's eyes as he had looked at her. She had felt slightly menaced by it, and briefly afraid of him. Black men did sometimes rape white women, and were hanged for it if they were caught.

A little nervously, she asked Becky, 'What did you tell him?'

'I told him to bugger off. Boys!'

Candy smiled at the contempt in her tone. Then, as Becky turned away to open her cold drink, Candy sneaked a look down at herself. Was she really sexy? As far as she knew, nobody had ever found her so before. Of course her nose was a bit too long – she had a complex about that. But maybe her figure wasn't so bad, after all.

She glanced at Becky, wondering if she had a boyfriend; she certainly gave the impression that she had had a lot of experience with boys. Candy wanted to ask her, but she was afraid that if she did, Becky might then ask *her* the same question. Rolling up her sleeves to make the most of the sunlight, Candy leaned back, sipping her cold drink thoughtfully.

Time was getting on; her father would be arriving soon. Before he did, she must try to arrange to see Becky again. But how should she broach the subject? Suddenly, she had an idea.

Sitting up, she said, 'Tell me, what language were you and that boy talking?'

'Sotho.'

'Are you a Sotho then?'

'I'm a Zulu,' Becky said proudly. 'But I can speak lots of languages. Zulu, Xhosa, Sotho, some Swazi . . .' She counted them on her fingers. 'What else? . . . English, Afrikaans . . .' As Candy pursed her lips admiringly, Becky asked, 'And you?'

'I can only speak English,' Candy confessed.

'You can't even speak Afrikaans?' Becky pretended to be shocked. 'The other official language? But you have to learn it at school.'

'I know. But I still can't speak it. It's probably because I don't like it,' Candy added in defence.

'I hate it,' Becky said violently. 'It's the language of oppression; of policemen, government officials; all those people who think because you're black you're a *bobbejaan*,* and should crawl round on all fours in front of them and lick their boots and be kicked in the backside. "Yes baas, no baas, kiss your arse, baas." ' She gave a loud, sarcastic snort. But as the fierceness went out of her eyes, she looked at Candy slightly

* *baboon*

anxiously, as if she was afraid that she might have said too much.

Taken aback by the unexpected outburst, Candy had no immediate reply.

Becky snatched up her empty cold drink can and started fiddling with it. 'Can you squash this with your bare hands?' she demanded.

'I shouldn't think so,' Candy said with an uneasy smile.

'Neither can I,' Becky admitted, causing them both to laugh.

'Listen,' Candy said suddenly, 'I was wondering . . . I mean . . . you see, I've always wanted to learn Zulu, and I was wondering . . . I wanted to ask you if you'd consider teaching me?'

'*You* want to learn Zulu?'

'Yes. Why not? I've always wished I could speak . . . well, any African language really, but particularly Zulu. And being Zulu yourself, you could teach me much better than anyone who wasn't.'

'*Yebo.*'

'What?'

'*Yebo.* That's Zulu for yes.'

'You'll teach me then?'

'Okay. For sure. Why not?'

'Of course I'll pay you,' Candy said hastily. 'And . . .'

But Becky cut her short. 'We're friends,' she reminded her. 'So I'll teach you for nothing.'

'No. Certainly not.' Candy shook her head vehemently. Wanting to help Becky financially was part of her motive. But she couldn't tell Becky that. Searching her mind frantically for a convincing argument, she went on, 'I must pay you because . . . because, well, I'm basically very lazy, you see. We've got to make it a proper business arrangement on a regular basis; otherwise I won't take it seriously and work hard enough. I know me. I'm like that, I'm afraid.'

'Okay. When do you want to start?'

'As soon as possible.'

'We can start now if you like.'

'Have a heart. I can see you're going to be a real tyrant of a teacher. Anyway, this is a bit public, isn't it? I wouldn't be able to concentrate properly.'

'Where then?' Becky asked pointedly.

Candy hadn't yet thought that far. However, it didn't take her long to realize there was only one place where the two of them could meet regularly in privacy, and that was her own home. She hesitated, uncertain how her parents would react to the idea. There was no logical reason why her parents should have any objections: they didn't support the government; they had always denounced its apartheid policies and insisted that the colour of a person's skin was irrelevant. Nevertheless, some instinct warned Candy that despite all this, they weren't exactly going to welcome Becky into their house with open arms.

She tried to push the prompting aside. Surely, once her parents had actually met Becky and seen for themselves how nice she was, they wouldn't mind Candy making friends with her. Candy remembered her mother saying more than once that if only all the children, from all the different races and cultures and language groups in the country, were sent to the same schools, and mixed together in the classroom and on the playground, there would be more hope of a peaceful future for them all.

Aware that Becky was looking at her expectantly, Candy made up her mind. 'I know,' she said brightly, as if an answer had only just occurred to her. 'We could have the lessons in my bedroom at home. I've got a large desk and we won't be disturbed there.'

When Becky didn't reply, Candy rushed on, 'I'm afraid it will be quite a long way for you to have to travel. I'll pay for your train and bus fares, of course, to make up for the inconvenience to you.'

'Where do you live?'

Just then, Candy caught sight of a blue Cortina moving slowly along the kerbside and identified her father at the wheel, frowning through the window as he searched for his daughter among the figures sitting alone or in little groups around the park. She waved wildly, glad of the excuse not to answer Becky's question. The fact that she lived in one of the exclusive northern suburbs of Johannesburg had suddenly become embarrassing to her.

After a few seconds her father spotted her and made desperate signals with his hand, which Candy interpreted to mean he was going to drive round the block to find parking.

'My dad's here,' she announced unnecessarily, for Becky had already scrambled to her feet and was hurriedly brushing the grass off her skirt.

'I must go,' she told Candy.

'Wait . . Hold on, we haven't settled anything. We don't even know how to get in touch with each other.' Candy wasn't altogether surprised that Becky wanted to get away before her father arrived, but she wanted the two of them to meet. It would make it easier to talk to her father about Becky later.

Becky grinned nervously. 'You'll be okay now,' she said. 'And I must run like a rabbit to catch my train. If you give me your address, I'll write and ask you when you want me to come and give you your first Zulu lesson. Okay?'

'Okay.' Candy tried to hide her disappointment as she delved into her bag for a pen. She carefully printed her address, and then added her telephone number, before folding up the page torn from her diary and giving it to Becky.

Without looking at it, Becky tucked it safely away in her pocket. 'I hope your ankle gets better very soon,' she said. 'Don't forget, not so many drinks next time, hey?'

'I'll try to remember.'

They smiled at each other, feeling shy again now that they were about to part.

Hoping to delay Becky as long as possible, Candy said, 'Listen, how about letting me have your address as well. Then we'll both know how to get in touch.'

When Becky had given her back her diary, Candy pretended to have difficulty deciphering the hasty scribble. 'What's this word? Orlando?'

Becky nodded impatiently.

'But that's not Soweto, is it?'

'Orlando is one of the locations in Soweto. Soweto is a big place, you know. I think there are twenty-six locations altogether. . . . You know nothing about Soweto, do you?'

Her tone was bantering, but Candy felt suddenly irritably defensive.

'How am I supposed to know anything when I'm not allowed into the township? I'm not going to be given a permit just to go and see what it's really like, am I?'

'You could always go on one of the official bus tours for tourists,' Becky teased. 'They'll take you to see the "nice" houses in Dube location, where the "rich" African businessmen live, and then they'll give you a nice cup of tea in the Ernest Oppenheimer Park.'

'And after my nice cup of tea I'll know all about Soweto,' Candy said sarcastically.

Becky grinned. 'For sure. You'll know all about nothing about Soweto.'

Out of the corner of her eye, Candy saw her father hurrying towards them across the park. To stop Becky noticing him, she said, 'Maybe you could smuggle me in one day.' She wasn't being serious; the very thought was rather terrifying.

'Maybe. One day . . . Hey! I must run now.'

However, she had left it too late; Candy's father had come up behind her. 'What have you done to yourself?' he called out to Candy.

25

Becky spun round and immediately stepped aside, separating herself from the other two.

'Hallo, Dad,' Candy said. 'Dad, this is Becky,' she went on quickly. 'She's been helping me and looking after me.'

'Oh.' He turned and glanced at Becky, who dipped her head in shy acknowledgement.

'Good afternoon, sir,' she said politely.

'Uh . . . hallo.' He was already bending down to look at Candy's ankle. 'It's rather swollen,' he commented. 'I hope you haven't broken it.'

'No, it's just a sprain, Dad. But Becky here has . . .'

'Is it very painful?'

Candy shook her head impatiently, aware that Becky had retreated a little further away and was fidgeting indecisively.

'Dad!' she said firmly. 'Becky has been absolutely marvellous. I don't know what I would have done without her.'

'Oh.' He cast a cursory smile in Becky's direction. 'That was very kind of her,' he said. 'Now, do you think you'll be able to walk as far as the car?'

Candy nodded once, sharply, scowling up at him in disappointment. He was letting her down badly. He could at least show some interest in Becky and address her directly. Trying not to appear too obvious, Candy pulled a face at him, indicating Becky with her eyes.

'What? . . . Oh yes, of course.'

Too late, Candy realized he had misunderstood her. Digging his hand into his pocket, he was already approaching Becky.

'Here,' he said, 'this is for being so kind and looking after my daughter until I got here,' and he held a one rand note out to her.

Helplessly, Candy stared at them both, red with shame. Anything she said now could only make the situation worse. She felt furious with her father, and yet she knew she couldn't altogether blame him for misunderstanding her. One glance

26

at Becky was enough to confirm her poverty, and under most circumstances white people would automatically expect to tip Africans for any assistance. But after everything that had passed between her and Becky, offering Becky money could only seem an insult.

Candy couldn't bear to watch, but she had to. She saw Becky look up and slowly begin to shake her head.

'Come on, take it,' Candy's father urged. 'You can buy yourself a treat, or some lunch perhaps, to make up for all the time and trouble you've taken.'

For a few seconds Becky continued to stare at him. Then slowly she stretched out her hand and allowed him to thrust the money into it.

'Thank you,' she said with careful politeness.

'Not at all, thank *you*,' he muttered, and as he turned away and started back towards Candy, she saw that his cheeks were pinker than usual.

Becky also had turned away, and afraid that she was going to rush off without even saying goodbye, Candy called out to her, 'Will you write to me soon?'

Becky stopped. 'Okay,' she said, and then she swung round and quickly disappeared among the people thronging the sidewalk.

Candy remained reflectively silent beside her father as he manoeuvred somewhat irritably through the congested city centre. Concentrating on his driving, he seemed unaware of her silence until they were through the worst of the traffic and speeding northwards along the M1 motorway. Then he turned and inspected her briefly.

'Are you all right?' he asked. 'You're not feeling faint or anything?'

'No. I'm okay,' Candy said abruptly.

'You look a bit white.'

'I'm okay . . . thanks.'

He glanced at her again, but said nothing further for a while.

She wanted to tell him he had embarrassed her, but she didn't want to upset him. After all, she was grateful to him for having come all the way into town to fetch her and for being so concerned about her. Nevertheless, she still couldn't help feeling slightly cross with him, and with herself. She was only just beginning to realize how complacent she had always been; how much for granted she had always taken her own life-style and privileged status within society.

If only her father would say something about Becky, so that she could talk to him about her. After what had happened, Candy felt it was up to him to mention Becky first. She expected it of him, to make up for his earlier negligence.

She stole a look at him. He was frowning at the road ahead, obviously immersed in his own thoughts. No doubt he was thinking about his beloved garden, fretting to get back into his old baggy trousers and potter about with a trowel or a pair of secateurs. With a silent sigh, she leaned back and stared through the window.

They had turned off the motorway and were taking one of her father's habitual routes through the quiet, grass-verged streets of a select suburb bordering their own. Each house was individually grand, set well back in its large grounds and surrounded by lush shrubbery and carefully tended flower beds. Life in such a suburb was both secluded and luxurious. The white families who lived here enjoyed every comfort, waited on by their black servants who looked after the garden, cleaned the house, did the cooking and washing and acted as nanny to the children, leaving their white 'masters' and 'madams' free to indulge their leisure as they fancied.

They were the nameless ones, these servants: impersonal shadows who moved back and forth behind the white foreground, doing all the chores essential for keeping the household running smoothly, at night retiring to their brick-walled rooms which usually abutted the garage at the side or back of the house, where they might entertain a friend for an evening but were prevented by law from having their families live with them.

Candy began thinking about Tom, her own family's African servant, who had been a member of the household since Candy was a baby. He had a wife, living on a reserve some sixty miles north of Johannesburg, and children – the youngest was roughly Candy's age. But he hardly ever saw them. He had watched Candy grow up from babyhood while his own children had grown up elsewhere without him.

It seemed incredible to Candy that he didn't resent her, or appear to harbour any bitterness. She had asked him once whether he minded not being able to have his wife live with him.

'Well . . .' He had grinned philosophically. 'What can you do? You can't do nothing about it.'

'But does it bother you?'

'Of course, Miss Candy. What you think?'

That was when she had asked him to stop calling her 'Miss'. 'Just call me Candy,' she had said.

'Why, Miss Cand?'

'Because . . . it's not necessary. Because . . . well, it makes me feel very old.'

'You are very old now, Miss Cand,' he had teased her, chuckling.

Guiltily, Candy suddenly realized that, along with everything else in her life, she had always taken Tom's particular role completely for granted. He had played an important part – even if a largely uncredited one – in her upbringing. She remembered how gentle and patient he had been with her as a child. He had never once scolded her, although often she must have been extremely irritating, clambering all over him and endlessly getting in his way as he went about his daily chores. One of her favourite games had been to ride him like a horse when he was down on his hands and knees, scrubbing or polishing the floors.

29

Her mother had told her that when she was still a baby and her mother couldn't stop her crying, she would hand her over to Tom. Apparently he would carry her out into the garden, crooning softly to her as he wandered about, finding 'nice *goggas*'* to show her. 'After I had spent ages trying to calm you, he would have you gurgling and chortling in no time,' her mother had confessed sheepishly.

Candy closed her eyes, then opened them again, startled, as the car braked unexpectedly. A boy on a bicycle had shot out of a driveway just ahead of them.

'Stupid idiot,' her father muttered.

They weren't far from home now. Candy looked at the familiar hedgerows, blinking against the occasional glare from the surface of swimming pools, half-hidden behind the thick foliage. Suddenly it all seemed strangely unreal: the blue sky, the smart houses gleaming white through the trees, the swimming pools, the tennis courts, the sweeping, neatly edged lawns. The early afternoon stillness was disquieting; it was as if the whole suburb was under a deep spell of sleep.

'It's like a big, green cocoon,' Candy thought, 'enclosing us all in our cosy, insulated life-style.'

She tried to form a clear picture of Becky's house in Soweto. But she could only get a hazy image, based on a distant view of the township. She had driven past Soweto only once, and she could still recall the mixture of fear and curiosity with which she had gazed at the ghetto, stretching endlessly across the barren veld like an uncontrolled attack of acne, oozing a yellowish-grey smog which discoloured the sky as far as the eye could see.

The monotonous hum of activity emanating from the township had made Candy feel uneasy; it had sounded almost as if the ghetto itself was groaning as it suppurated into the sky. At the time, she had shivered involuntarily, finding the view eerily depressing.

* *insects*

Now, however, she found herself feeling a lot more curious about Soweto. She would still be terrified to go there, but she felt that if it were possible she would like to visit Becky in her home and see for herself what township life was like. But it wasn't possible. She wasn't likely to be given an entry permit for a social visit. And she didn't think she would ever be brave enough to try to sneak into Soweto without one.

She glanced at her father. They were almost home and still he hadn't mentioned Becky.

He turned just then, and noticing her glum expression, said reassuringly, 'We're nearly there. Then you can put your feet up. That should ease the pain.' When Candy didn't say anything, he added, 'Poor old thing. You must have come a terrible cropper.'

Candy couldn't help smiling. It wasn't usual for him to talk like that.

'Oh, by the way,' he went on casually after a moment, 'did I hear you asking that girl to write to you?'

'You mean Becky?'

'That's right. The African girl who helped you.'

'Why?'

'Did you give her our address?'

'Yes, I did. Why?'

He shrugged. 'I'm not sure that was a very wise thing to do. You don't know her at all. I'm not suggesting she's necessarily up to no good herself, but she might pass our address and whatever other information you gave her on to somebody else. The townships are riddled with young thugs, you know, and some of them have become very professional in their operations. They act on information and know exactly when to strike, cleaning you out of everything you possess. And heaven help you if you're unlucky enough to be there. Just the other week a woman was stabbed to death by a black youth who had broken into her house.' He shook his head worriedly. 'You really can't be too careful these days.'

Candy's heart jolted nervously. Had she done the wrong thing? What if their house was broken into and they were all murdered because of her? Briefly she was gripped by a feeling of terror, imagining herself waking up at night to see a black man climbing through her bedroom window with a knife in his hand. It was an image that had haunted her frequently as a child.

But no, she couldn't believe Becky would mean her any harm. She wasn't going to let her father frighten her unnecessarily. To allay his own fears, she told him about the five rand note she had given Becky to go and buy them both a snack.

'She could have run off with it, couldn't she?' she pointed out. 'It's not as if I only gave her some change. To her, five rand is probably quite a lot of money.'

Her father merely grunted as he changed gear and slowed down to turn into the driveway of their house.

'Actually, Dad . . . I asked her to write to me so that we could arrange to meet again. She's going to give me Zulu lessons. You know how much I've always wanted to . . .' Candy stopped, aware that he wasn't listening to her.

Frowning as he pulled on the handbrake, he said, 'I really must do something about that hydrangea today. It hasn't been looking at all happy recently.'

2

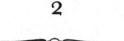

'Happy birthday, Dad,' Candy said, hobbling into the dining-room with a present tucked rather selfconsciously under one arm.

Her father looked up from his newspaper and hastily wiped his mouth as she bent to kiss him on the cheek.

'What's this then?' he asked, pretending to be surprised as she thrust the large, thin package into his lap.

'I'm afraid it's not very much. I couldn't go shopping because of my ankle, so I had to settle for making you something instead.'

A little nervously, she watched him peel off the blue crinkly paper. She had been so pleased with her painting when she had finished it. Her roses actually looked like roses, and she thought she had reproduced the soft sheen on the petals rather well. But now, as she saw her father hold out the cardboard-framed picture and study it thoughtfully, she was filled with sudden doubt.

'It's really jolly good. That bud is my Madam Butterfly all right. The colouring is perfect. How did you know it was one of my favourites?' He looked at her, smiling and shaking his head in a rare display of paternal pride.

Candy glowed. It wasn't often she experienced a particular closeness to her father, but when she did, the fresh discovery of the bond between them always overwhelmed her a little, hidden as it generally was by his somewhat gruff reserve and her shyness.

'Turn it round, Ron, so I can see,' her mother said. '. . . Oh yes, it is lovely, isn't it. The roses look so real, and I like the way you've caught the reflections in the vase.'

Colin sneered. 'So that's what it's meant to be. I thought it was a sausage with gangrene.'

Ignoring Colin, Candy's father carefully laid the painting, face upwards, on the sideboard behind him.

'I'll hang it in the study when I get home this evening,' he told Candy. 'In pride of place over my desk,' he added. And he smiled at her again in a way which left both of them feeling too embarrassed to say anything more to each other.

Candy took her place at the table and helped herself to toast. She avoided looking at Colin who was sitting directly opposite her.

'Any more tea going?' her father asked after a few moments, reappearing briefly from behind his newspaper.

Automatically, Candy picked up his empty cup and passed it across to her mother.

'Pour Dad a cup will you, dear, while I sort through the rest of this mail . . . Why, here's one for you.'

'Me?' Surprised, Candy took the envelope from her mother. Immediately she knew it must be from Becky. Nobody else she knew would have written the address in pencil. Inside was a piece of lined paper which had obviously been torn from an exercise book. She unfolded it on her lap so that Colin, who was watching her curiously, wouldn't be able to read it.

'Dear Candy, I hope your ankle is now very well again. Did you take some castor oil? I am writing to you because I have to come to Johannesburg on Saturday to buy more Easter eggs. The other ones got sat on by a fat man in the train going home. It's the truth. He was very cross because the chocolate stuck to his trousers. But it's no matter. He is not a very nice man I think. Some people who know him call him *unwabu* (that means a chameleon) because they say he changes his colour when he talks to the police. They think he is a spy. If you can also come to the city on Saturday, maybe we can meet at the same place in the park. I will look for you

34

there at 11 o'clock (in the morning, hey, not in the evening). *Sala kahle*, Becky Mpala. (*Sala kahle* means *stay well* in Zulu.)'

'Who's your letter from, dear?' Candy's mother asked.

Candy folded the letter and slipped it into its envelope. 'Oh, it's just from the girl I met in town last Saturday,' she said.

'Which girl, dear?'

'You know, the one who helped me.'

'You mean the African girl?'

'Becky,' Candy said, nodding.

'Oh . . .' Her mother put down her cup. 'Why is she writing to you, dear?'

Candy hesitated. She hadn't yet spoken to her mother about the Zulu lessons and about Becky visiting their house. She had been waiting to catch her in the right mood, and breakfast was not a good time, especially with Colin there. She knew how he would react to the idea.

But her mother was looking at her expectantly, so Candy said, 'She's written to find out how my ankle is.'

'Really? How very thoughtful of her.'

Candy shrugged. 'She seems a very nice girl.'

'What did you say her name was again?'

'Becky. It's short for Rebecca.'

'And she's the one who helped you when you fell?'

'If it wasn't for her, I'd probably have been trampled to death,' Candy exaggerated.

Her mother shook her head sadly. 'People just don't care any more, do they?'

'Becky did,' Candy was quick to point out.

'Yes, well . . .' Her mother brightened. 'One can draw heart from that, at least. It does seem to show that this dratted government of ours hasn't totally succeeded in destroying all signs of goodwill between the races.'

Candy saw her chance. But still she hesitated, glancing uncertainly at Colin. He was leaning forward on the table, his head down, apparently absorbed in the latest issue of a

35

sports magazine he subscribed to. Her father seemed to be similarly engrossed in his newspaper. Suddenly, Candy thought how ridiculous it was to be nervous of saying that she was going to see Becky again; as if she was admitting to something slightly shameful. Apart from anything else, it was an insult to Becky's trust in impulsively declaring the two of them to be friends. That decided Candy.

In a firm voice, she said, 'Actually, Becky also wrote to suggest meeting me again in town on Saturday.'

'Oh.' Her mother looked surprised. 'Why does she want to do that?'

'It was my idea in the first place. *I* wanted to see her again. I asked her to write to me so we could fix up a time.' Candy raised her chin defiantly and stared straight into her mother's eyes. 'I've also asked her to teach me Zulu.'

Her mother lowered her gaze and began flicking through the small pile of opened mail lying next to her plate. 'That's very nice, dear,' she said distantly.

Candy watched her, waiting. Finally, her mother looked up frowning, and took off her reading glasses.

'You've asked this girl to teach you Zulu?'

'That's right. She's an ideal person, being a Zulu herself. It's tremendous luck to have found someone suitable at last. She offered to teach me for nothing, but obviously I must pay her. I've been wanting to talk to you about that.' Candy paused hopefully. As her mother remained silent, she went on, 'I could pay for the lessons out of my pocket money, if you like.'

She saw her mother glance towards her father, but he remained hidden behind his newspaper. 'Perhaps Becky could teach you Zulu as well, Mum,' she suggested cunningly. Her mother was always saying how much she wished she could speak an African language.

Her mother laughed. 'I'm much too old now to start learning a new language. My brains have become far too addled after all these years.'

36

'Nonsense!' Candy grinned. 'You should think about it seriously. But anyway, you can always see how I get on first. I want to start as soon as possible.' She pushed her plate away and leaned back in her chair, trying to project a cheerful confidence she was far from feeling.

It was obvious that her mother was being evasive. Candy had a nasty feeling that the next few minutes were going to be even more difficult than she had suspected. However, now she had got this far, she knew she had to go on. It was better to get the whole thing over and done with as soon as possible.

Her mother, meanwhile, had started fiddling with the pile of mail again. Extracting a bill, she pretended to study it in great detail, her brow furrowed in exaggerated concentration. Candy stared at her until she had to look up.

'Well . . .?' Candy asked.

'Well what, dear?'

'Don't you think it's a good idea, my having Zulu lessons?'

'Of course I do, dear. I think it's an excellent idea, if you're really serious about it. Only . . .' Her mother smiled a little anxiously.

'Only?' Candy prompted.

'Well, how can you be sure this girl would be able to teach you properly? I mean it's not as if you know her at all, do you?'

'I've told you she's a Zulu, which is the important thing. I also know she's intelligent, that she's interesting to talk to and that I like her and want to get to know her better. Isn't that enough?'

Her mother nodded doubtfully. 'And where would she teach you?'

Candy swallowed. 'That's one of the things I wanted to talk to you about. Obviously she would have to come here. There's really no other place where we could meet in privacy. I was thinking we could have the lessons in my bedroom –

we wouldn't disturb anybody there. But I'd really need to have a lesson every week, otherwise I wouldn't make much progress.'

A sudden silence fell over the table. Candy was aware that her father had stopped reading, although his newspaper remained raised, shielding his face from her view. Nobody moved. Then Colin turned over a page of his magazine and casually went on reading, and Candy breathed out in relief to know that he, at least, seemed unaware of what she had said.

Her mother began picking crumbs off the cloth in quick, nervous movements. 'I don't know, dear,' she said. 'I really don't know. I mean I'm not even sure the law allows it.' She glanced desperately at her husband, but the newspaper blocked her appeal for help. Raising her voice, she asked, 'Is it legal, Ron, do you know?'

There was a pause, and then Candy's father laid the paper aside irritably.

'Don't ask me,' he said. 'As far as I know, you can have Africans visit you so long as you don't offer them liquor.'

'There's no problem then.' Candy gave a feeble grin. 'I shouldn't think Becky would expect anything stronger than tea.'

'It's not all that simple and straightforward, dear.' Her mother shifted uncomfortably in her chair. 'There are the neighbours to consider. I mean, what are they going to say when they find out you have a black friend visiting you regularly on a . . .'

'Bugger the neighbours.'

'*What* did you say?'

Candy turned and looked at her father in nervous, silent defiance.

'I won't have you talking that way to your mother,' he warned. Angrily, he picked up his newspaper and hid behind it once more.

Candy shrugged. She had half-expected this reaction from her parents, but she still couldn't help feeling bitterly disappointed in them. It didn't help her to notice that Colin had straightened up and was now staring round the table in surprise.

'What's going on?' he demanded.

Before her mother could answer, Candy said in a barely controlled voice, 'I don't see that it's got anything to do with the neighbours, Mum. Anyway, even if they did see Becky come and go, they'd simply assume she was visiting Tom.'

'And that's another thing, dear. You have to consider Tom in all this. How do you imagine he'd feel, being expected to serve tea or whatever to a black girl young enough to be his grand-daughter? You know what African men are like. They consider their women to be subordinate and expect to be served by them, not the other way round.'

Candy shook her head in exasperation.

'What's all this about a black . . .'

'For goodness sake, Mum. Surely you don't think I'm so helpless that I can't make a cup of tea myself for Becky. I wouldn't dream of expecting Tom to serve us.'

'Who the hell is this Becky you're . . .'

'Never mind Tom feeling embarrassed or humiliated,' Candy went on hurriedly. 'How do you imagine I'd feel? Tom's the last person I'd want to parade in front of Becky in his white kitchen suit.'

'But don't you see? . . .' Her mother sighed patiently. 'That's exactly what I'm trying to make you understand about all this. You know, and I know, that the laws in this country are ridiculous . . . insane . . . But because of the way things are, you just can't do what you like without first carefully considering the possible consequences for other people. I mean, have you thought what might happen to this black girl if . . .'

'Becky. Her name is Becky, Mum,' Candy insisted crossly.

39

'Becky, yes . . . well, have you considered what could happen to her if someone was to complain to the police about her visiting our house regularly? You know what the police are like when it comes to dealing with black people.'

'You mean to tell me you've invited a coon girl to this house?' Colin asked incredulously.

'It's none of your blasted business.'

'None of my business? You bet your backside it is. What the hell do you think you're up to now? Trying to cultivate coons as comrades like the commies?'

Candy's face went white with suppressed anger. 'Why don't you go to work and get there on time for once,' she suggested as sarcastically as she could.

Colin merely laughed. 'Inviting coons to tea, indeed. Next you'll be wanting to marry one. Mind you,' he shrugged, 'who else would want you?'

'Don't talk like that,' his mother scolded. 'It isn't nice.'

'Well, honestly, Ma, the girl's a nutter. I mean, I always knew she was a sissie, but I didn't realize she was a *kaffirsussie** to boot.'

Candy struggled to control herself. 'So what if I am,' she snapped. 'You know what you are, don't you? You're nothing but a . . .'

'Stop it! At once! you two.' Candy's father slammed down his newspaper suddenly with such force that they all jumped involuntarily. Glaring furiously at Colin, he said, 'You sound just like a *jaap*.† It's about time you pulled yourself together and developed some adult sense, instead of talking like an ignorant imbecile.'

Candy ducked her head to hide her smile. Her father had said exactly what she wanted to say herself. Colin scraped back his chair and stood up, grinning.

'You see, Dad,' he said cheerfully. 'The trouble is I in-

* *kaffir sister* (someone considered to be too friendly towards Africans)
† *yokel*

40

herited Ma's beauty and your brains.' As he went past his father he gave him a playful punch on the arm. 'Have a happy birthday. I must be off,' and he walked gaily out of the room.

His father glowered. 'Insolent young pup,' he muttered. But Candy saw his lips twitch slightly as he met her mother's eyes across the table.

'Don't forget to put a hot compress on your face before you go,' Candy's mother called out to Colin. She was always trying to get him to do something about his acne. 'Shall I come and do it for you?'

Colin's face appeared briefly round the doorway. 'You leave my cookie chasers alone,' he told her. 'They're my only protection against being raped by all the girls in my office.'

His mother giggled. 'Don't you believe . . .' she began, then stopped as she saw he had already gone. 'Of course, he won't listen to me,' she added to no one in particular.

'I'd better get a move on.' Candy's father stood up and folded his newspaper. 'If you're coming with me,' he told Candy, 'I'll be leaving in five minutes or so and I don't want to be kept waiting.'

'I'll be ready.'

As soon as he had left the room, Candy's mother started collecting plates together noisily. Candy waited to see if she would refer to their earlier conversation first. When she didn't, Candy said irritably, 'What about it then, Mum?'

'What about what, dear? . . . I wonder where Tom's got to with the tray. Would you mind going and . . .'

'Mum!'

'What? . . . Oh yes, you were saying . . .?'

'Is it, or is it not all right for Becky to come to our house to give me Zulu lessons?'

Her mother leaned across the table to pick up a dirty serviette. 'I've already told you, I really don't think it's a very good idea, not because I . . .'

41

'You! . . . Of all people! I would have expected you to be the first to . . .' Candy couldn't go on.

The ridge of her mother's cheeks reddened, and for a few moments she too seemed unable to speak. Finally, she managed a small, hurt, angry smile.

'There really isn't time to discuss it properly now,' she said. 'Can't it wait until this evening when I've had a chance to think about it?'

'No!' Candy was all too familiar with her mother's delaying tactics. 'I just can't see what all the fuss is about,' she said stubbornly. 'Finally, I've met an African girl of my own age, and . . . I'd like to get to know her better. What's wrong with that?'

'Nothing. Nothing at all. I'm all for it, as you know. But what you don't seem to understand is . . .' Her mother broke off suddenly as Tom appeared in the doorway. 'It's all right, Tom, we've finished. You can come and clear the table now, thank you.'

Looking relieved, she turned back to Candy. 'Don't worry, I'm sure we'll be able to sort something out,' she said soothingly. 'But you really ought to hurry up now. You know how Dad hates to be kept waiting.'

Candy stood her ground. 'If you won't let Becky come to our house, then we'll just have to meet somewhere else. I'll be seeing her in town this Saturday anyway, but I had been hoping to arrange a date for her to come here.' Ignoring her mother's anxious glances in Tom's direction, she went on, 'After all, she did go out of her way to help me when I hurt my ankle. At the very least I would have thought it only decent to invite her to tea to say thank you.'

She was about to say more when her mother grasped her arm and pulled her through the open french windows on to the patio.

'I wish you wouldn't speak like that in front of Tom,' her mother grumbled. 'It's so embarrassing.'

42

Candy shrugged, unrepentant.

'Look, I'll tell you what . . .' her mother continued, smiling in a conciliatory way as she picked a stray hair off Candy's school blazer. 'Perhaps you could invite this girl . . . Becky . . . to come here one Sunday afternoon when Tom's off. Goodness knows what the neighbours will think, but I suppose it will be all right.'

'How about this Sunday?' Candy asked, beginning to smile herself.

'I don't know . . . I'm not sure this Sunday is a good idea.'

'Why not?'

'Oh well, I suppose it will be all right.'

Candy heard her father call out impatiently from the passage.

'I'm coming,' she shouted. 'I'm ready.' She hadn't brushed her teeth, but that didn't matter. She gave her mother a brief, tight hug. "Bye Mum . . . take care.'

"Bye dear. Don't forget your sandwiches.'

Glancing back from the doorway, Candy was suddenly struck by the visible signs of ageing in her mother as she stood staring pensively across the garden. Her shoulders were stooped, and the flesh around her chin was beginning to sag. It was the first time Candy had noticed a change in her mother's appearance and it disturbed her painfully, provoking a pang of conscience as well as something else – a fierceness of feeling rooted far back in her childhood. She was half-tempted to go and give her mother another hug when her father appeared behind her.

'Come on,' he complained. 'I thought you said you were ready.'

'I am.'

She grabbed her briefcase from the corner of the hall; and as she limped ahead of him out to the garage, she was aware of feeling older herself, and of being prepared to take responsibility for her convictions, whatever might be involved.

*   *   *

Tom's large, broad hands, grooved with wrinkles like over-used wrapping paper, peeled the potatoes with a skill acquired from many years of practice. Perched on the edge of the kitchen table, Candy watched fascinated as the long, delicate, curling strips appeared between the thick fingers, making her think of snakes as they slithered down into the chipped enamel bowl, already half-filled with vegetable scraps.

After a while, Candy's gaze shifted with her thoughts to settle on Tom's face. She studied his familiar features with a tenderness she could not express in words. She knew that she loved him, but it would have sounded strange to have said as much aloud.

Instead, she asked, 'How is the hole in your head today, Tom?'

'It's all right, Miss Cand.'

'Then why have you got cottonwool in it? Is it hurting?'

'No. There's some pus, that's all.' He wrinkled up his nose. 'It's not very nice for everybody to see, so I cover it up.' Noticing how worried she looked, he added, grinning, 'It means maybe the rain's coming now.'

'I think you should see a doctor,' Candy told him firmly.

'Doctor? What you think a doctor can do, Miss Cand? Doctors don't know nothing about spells. A witch-doctor maybe.'

She sighed, smiling. 'So now it's a spell, is it?'

'What, Miss Cand?'

'That caused the hole in your head.'

He chuckled, but gave no answer as he went on working. Candy leaned forward to peer more closely at the small, round indentation in his skull, directly above his right ear. It was strange because it was so neat. It looked as if a thumb had been carefully pushed into the bone while it was still soft, forming a little hollow without breaking or even scarring the skin. What made it all the more fascinating was the com-

44

plete mystery of its origin. Countless times Candy had asked Tom how he had got it, only to be given a different explanation each time: a *tsotsi* had hit him with an iron pole; he had tripped over something when he was a young boy and bashed his head on a stone; it had just happened one night while he was asleep; or – and this was the story which had most impressed Candy – he had once been caught by the *tokoloshe* and in the ensuing struggle, the nasty little spirit had tried to poke his eye out. Tom had ducked and the *tokoloshe's* finger had drilled a dent in his skull instead.

Candy had long since stopped believing she would ever learn the truth of the matter. But it worried her to know that the wound, whatever its cause, was still festering after all these years.

'Tom,' she said, 'you know you really ought to go and see a doctor.'

'What for, Miss Cand? Don't you worry, I'm getting old, that's all. Nobody can do nothing about that. Look, I've got no teeth any more.' He showed her the gaps in the front of his mouth. 'And my eyes can't see now. Soon I must have "four eyes".'

Candy laughed, trying to imagine what he would look like in glasses.

'I'm plenty too much *madala** now, Miss Cand. Maybe I must die soon, I don't know.'

'Never!' She couldn't bear to think of him not being there. He had always been such a solidly dependable presence in her life.

She had a sudden urge to tell him how sorry she was for always having taken him so much for granted, and how much she regretted the many times she had thoughtlessly added to his laborious task of keeping the house clean and tidy. However, she remained silent from fear of embarrassing them both.

* *old*

45

As she watched him, she found herself trying to analyse him. He was almost illiterate, his knowledge was extremely limited. And yet, in his own simple way he was surprisingly wise, and he had a basic integrity that seemed incorruptible. She had sometimes noted a childlike quality in his expression, and now she suddenly realized why. In one sense he was a child. Not the child she remembered herself to have been – devious, manipulative – but the child of the Bible and moral fables: uncomplicated, undefiled, with a simple innocence derived from living in harmony with some natural law of right and wrong. But in every other sense he was a man, worthy of her respect and admiration. She squirmed a little in knowing she hadn't always treated him as one.

'What's the matter, Miss Cand? Why you looking at me like that?'

Candy blushed. 'Nothing . . . no reason. I was just thinking.'

'Ha.' He was shelling peas now, using one movement of his thumb to split the pods lengthways and spill their contents into a saucepan filled with water. The green pellets were hitting the surface with small, satisfying, plopping sounds.

'Tom . . . are you frightened of dying?'

He chuckled from deep down in his belly, causing the table edge to tremble slightly against the back of Candy's knees. 'What you think, Miss Cand? When you get old, you must die. You can't do nothing about that.'

'Yes, I know. But does it worry you – the thought of being dead, I mean?'

'Why? What's the use to worry? Death is curranteed. If you worry, worry, worry, the worms still eat you. Don't you say so, Miss Cand?'

'I suppose so.' Frowning, she leaned over and helped herself to a handful of peas.

'Hey, don't do that.'

'Anyway, you aren't going to die yet, so I don't know why we're talking like this.'

He glanced up at her, amused. 'How you know that?'

'Because you're too good to die yet, and because I don't know what I would do if you did.' She spoke jokingly; it was the closest she could come to telling him what she was feeling.

Laughing, he shook his head. 'No, it's no good, Miss Cand. I'm not going to make you trifle tonight. Look at the time already.'

After a moment's hesitation, Candy also laughed. 'Aw, go on,' she pleaded, finding some relief in falling back into their old familiar habit of light-hearted banter.

'No, no, no. There's plenty too much to do already.'

'What is for supper then?'

'Fried flying ants.' He often told her this, knowing he could count on her to react in disgust ever since he had first given her a detailed description of eating the insects when he was a boy.

'Urggh!' Candy slithered off the table. 'If you dare dish up those things for supper, I'll leave home – I mean it.'

'Good. And take all your books with you please. They make too much dust.'

'You'll miss me,' she called from the doorway, and heard his satisfied chuckle as she went back to her room to continue her English essay. She knew he would make her trifle now, as a surprise. Within the rigid rules of their relationship, it was one of the ways he could show his affection for her.

'The character of Hamlet can be interpreted in several different ways,' Candy wrote, and then stopped to watch a bee, loaded with pollen, buzzing desperately against the window pane.

'It's open higher up, you twit,' she told it, waiting to see whether it would find its own way out. When it didn't, she sighed and pushed up the lower half of the window, at the same time nudging the bee closer to the widening gap. For a

47

split second the insect seemed to hesitate before winging out into space and freedom, to be quickly lost in the general glaze of the mid-afternoon sunshine.

'The bee doesn't know it, but I just performed a miracle for it,' she mused, wondering solemnly whether individual human struggles were often as helplessly myopic as the bee's. Perhaps she could work that thought into the theme of her essay? She could certainly do with something to pad out the length.

The problem was she was feeling too restless to concentrate, even with so few obvious distractions around her. She couldn't imagine how Becky managed to work in such a small space, surrounded by people talking and doing things. Becky had told her that she did her homework in the kitchen, and that she stuffed tissues in her ears and tied a scarf round her head to shut out the worst of the noise.

'Was Hamlet unbalanced, or was he . . .?' What? Candy couldn't think of a suitably impressive alternative, so she drew a line through her unfinished sentence. The scratch of her pen sounded like a screech in the silence.

She found the stillness disturbing. The house seemed unnaturally quiet. Even the leaves on the tree outside the window appeared to be lifeless, hanging heavily on the branches like glistening drops of molten wax. It was as if the heat had suddenly transfixed time and nothing would ever stir again. Then she heard Tom moving about in the kitchen, humming softly to himself, and she breathed out thankfully.

The tune had a hymn-like quality, but she doubted its origin was religious. Tom was not a Christian because, as he had explained to her once, 'You tell me, Miss Cand, how you make a baby without a father? If God can make Jesus without a father, why He need a woman? He should make Jesus all by himself.'

Candy tried to picture herself introducing Becky to Tom. What would she say? And what would Becky and Tom say to each other? Candy could imagine the two of them finding something to talk about if they were left alone together, but not while she was there. It would all be very embarrassing, she was sure. She blushed at the thought of Tom referring to her as Miss Candy in front of Becky. 'I really must try to stop him calling me "Miss",' she decided, frowning down at the open page of the book in front of her.

'. . . Foul deeds will rise, though all the earth o'erwhelm them to men's eyes.'

Suddenly Candy was afraid, for herself as well as for Becky and Tom, seeing them all as Hamlets in their separate ways, caught up in a sinful system of suffering which they all seemed incapable of changing.

The sense of identity inspired her. Picking up her pen, she wrote, 'The character of Hamlet should be seen as a study of a personal crisis of conscience, courage and commitment'. And warming to her task, she was soon scribbling furiously.

*   *   *

''Scuse me, medem?'

Candy swung round to find Becky bowing, her hands pressed together in an obsequious gesture.

'Does medem need a wash girl, please medem? Very clean, very quick, very good wash girl, medem.'

Candy felt herself blushing. 'Oh . . . Hallo,' she said, screwing up her eyes painfully against the sun's glare as she tried to look up at Becky. 'I didn't see you coming.'

Becky laughed. Wriggling free of the satchel on her shoulders, she sank down on to the grass beside Candy.

'Whew! It's hot, hey?'

Candy nodded, and they smiled a little shyly at each other.

'I'm glad you could make it,' Candy said.

'Me too. I didn't think I would. The train was very very crowded. I got 99.999 per cent suffocated. It's the truth.' Becky giggled nervously. 'Hey! How is your ankle?'

'Oh, it's fine now. Almost completely better.'

'I'm very glad.'

They smiled at each other again, not knowing what to say next. After a moment, Candy picked up the plastic bag at her side and fished around in it.

'You must be thirsty,' she said. 'Here . . .' She produced two cans of Coke. 'This should help.'

'Ooohh! Thank you. I was beginning to feel like that instant milk you buy. You know . . . what's it called again? . . . Dehydrated.' Becky snapped the lid of the can open smartly, and raised it to her lips. 'One instant piccaninny coming up.'

Noticing that Candy was looking puzzled, Becky stopped drinking and pointed to the can. 'Water, see? And *Cocoa*-Cola for extra colouring. Pour into dehydrated piccaninny and hey presto! – instant midnight milk, brand name Becky. Doesn't go sour because it doesn't come from a cow. Manufactured in *So-where-to*? Third class, so very cheap – half-price. Colour fast guaranteed.' She laughed loudly, and after a moment so did Candy.

Then Candy looked away, pretending that something had caught her attention across the park. She didn't know what to make of Becky this morning. Candy wished she would stop joking about her colour and status. Becky might only be trying to be amusing, but she was making Candy feel embarrassed and uncomfortable.

Avoiding Becky's eye, Candy pulled some sandwiches out of the plastic bag. 'I've brought us something to eat as well,' she said, hearing the abruptness in her own voice. 'I hope you like cold beef and cucumber.'

'Yes. Thank you. I like anything,' Becky told her in a suddenly formal, polite tone.

Now I've made her feel uncomfortable, Candy thought, and for a few seconds she was painfully conscious of everything that stood between them. Hoping to make amends, she said flippantly, 'Anything? Even fried flying ants?'

To her relief, Becky's expression relaxed into its usual good humour.

'I don't know. I haven't tried any. But I've eaten dried mopane worms. They're okay. Nice and crunchy anyway.'

'Worms? . . . How could you?'

'Why not? They're meat, aren't they?'

'Well . . .'

'Do you like meat?' Becky asked.

'I'm not crazy about it,' Candy admitted.

'I love it.' Becky smacked her lips together loudly. 'I could eat it all the time if it wasn't so expensive.'

Candy was about to say, 'But it isn't,' and then stopped herself. She thought of her meals at home. Her family ate meat three times a day, every day. They wouldn't consider any meal – not even breakfast – to be a proper meal without it. She could imagine Colin's reaction, particularly, if her mother tried to introduce an occasional alternative.

She looked at Becky guiltily. 'How often do you have meat?' she asked.

'Maybe twice, three times a week, sometimes more when my uncle does well in the shop. Mostly we eat mealie-meal, soup, bread – we eat a lot of bread.'

'You ought to be fat on so much starch.' Candy tried to joke, but she was secretly horrified at how atrociously extravagant her own daily diet seemed by comparison. Afraid that Becky was going to ask her about it, she said, 'Do you use that for school?', and she pointed to the torn and tatty satchel lying on the grass between them.

Becky nodded. 'I've had it ever since I started,' she said proudly.

'What are schools like in Soweto?'

'Not so good. There are not so many – not nearly enough, and there are too many children in the classes to be able to learn properly. In lots of primary schools, the teachers have to give the same lessons over again in the afternoon to different children, but the classes are still too big. We call it the "hot seat" system because the seats stay warm all the time.' She laughed.

Candy shook her head in sympathy. 'But do you like school?' she asked. 'Apart from all that, I mean.'

'I like *learning*.' Becky gave her a meaningful look. 'Do you know about Bantu* Education?'

'What about it?' Candy hedged.

Becky grinned. 'My uncle calls it Brainwashing Evil. He tells me all the time not to believe what the government tries to teach us in our text books. But I know about the bias. I'm not stupid.'

'Yes,' Candy said. It hadn't ever occurred to her that her own school text books might be biased. She had resented having to study the Great Trek† over and over again in history, but she had never really questioned the validity of anything she was being taught. The sudden revelation of her gullibility shocked her into silence.

Becky, too, said nothing further until she had finished eating her sandwiches. Then she wiped her mouth with her hand and smiled at Candy with satisfaction.

'That was good,' she said. 'Oh well . . . school's okay, I suppose. I'm lucky really to be there still. Most children leave after Standard Two. My mother wants me to go on and take my matric. I'm in Form One now,' she added a little boastfully. 'And you?'

'Form Four.'

They stared at each other, showing their mutual surprise. Knowing that they were the same age, they had both obviously assumed they were at the same level in school.

* *African*
† Between 1834 and 1838 thousands of Boers ('farmers', the descendants of the first white Dutch, French and German settlers in the Cape) trekked north to escape from British rule.

'You must be very clever,' Becky decided, adding defensively, 'I haven't failed any year.'

'No, I'm not clever, honestly. Maybe your school system is different, maybe you start school later or something.'

'Maybe. Maybe we have to do more years in primary school. I don't know.' Becky shrugged. 'But you're so lucky – only one more year to go. I hope I can do my matric. I want to very much, but maybe it won't happen. I don't know.'

'Why ever not if your mother's happy to . . .?'

'Money . . .' Becky rubbed her fingers together. 'Money. It takes a lot of money to go to school. Maybe my mother won't have enough.'

'But why?'

'Because it takes more and more money all the time. Maybe my mother won't . . .'

'No, I mean, why should it cost a lot? After all, school's free.'

'Free?' Becky hooted. 'Maybe for you, but not for us.'

Candy stared at her open-mouthed. 'You're not serious? You mean you actually have to pay to go to school?'

'It's the truth. And then you have to buy your books and . . . ah-ah-ah, there are too many expenses.'

'Books! You have to pay for books as well? Doesn't your school supply them?'

'Some. But there are never enough. So if you want to do your work properly you have to go and buy your own.'

Candy continued to gaze at her disbelievingly.

'It's the truth.'

'Good God! But why? I don't understand it. I mean, how could the Government do it? It's . . . it's criminal.'

'You want me to tell you why?'

Candy nodded dumbly.

'It's simple. We mustn't be encouraged to become too educated. A little education makes us useful; too much education would make us too clever and "cheeky".'

53

Candy was silent. She did not want to accept what Becky was telling her, but she knew that she had to, because there was no other likely explanation for such discrimination. She felt her anger curdling into hatred, tasting sour with her shame at having to acknowledge her nationality.

'The bastards! . . .' was all she managed to say finally.

'Sshh! . . .' Becky warned, grinning. 'Big Ears are coming.'

Candy turned in the direction Becky was looking. Two policemen were ambling towards them along the path. Their eyes were hidden in the shadows cast by their peaked caps. However, Candy was sure they were looking straight at her, and her heart jerked a little. There was no reason why she should feel nervous; she wasn't breaking any law by sitting in the sunshine talking to a black person. Nevertheless, she sensed that Becky also had stiffened slightly and drawn away from her.

Lowering her face, Candy stared fixedly at her knees. She hated policemen; she despised them. They were nearly all Afrikaners which didn't help, and they were generally known to be utterly brutal in their dealings with Africans. She had no respect for their authority, but she was afraid of it, which was why she listened to the heavy, dull tramp of their approaching footsteps with trepidation.

From under her eyebrows she saw a pair of boots stop in front of her, and she looked up to find two pale blue eyes staring down at her coolly.

'*Môre.*'*

'*Môre,*' she replied guardedly, forcing herself to meet the policeman's metallic gaze.

'*Dis baie warm, nè ?*'

'Yes, it is very warm,' she agreed, pointedly speaking English, resentfully nervous of the way he was looking at her. Refusing to speak his language was as far as she dared go to show her disdain.

* '*Morning*

54

The corners of his stiff lips dented slightly. 'This is a nice park, hey?'

'Yes, it is.' She was sure he was leading up to something and she suddenly dreaded his next question.

However, he merely grunted, and turned his steel eyes to Becky. As if this was a signal his companion had been waiting for, he now stepped forward and gruffly asked Becky in Afrikaans how old she was.

'Fifteen,' Becky replied promptly in the same language.

'Stand up when you talk to me.'

Meekly, Becky obeyed him.

Candy glared at the deeply tanned face with its spiky moustache and pock-marked cheeks. She wanted to smash her fist into the thin mouth as the man scowled at Becky. But she couldn't do anything; she could only watch in helpless horror as 'blue eyes' now joined in.

'What have you got in there?' he demanded in Afrikaans, pointing to the satchel lying on the grass at Becky's feet.

'Books.'

He thrust out his hand impatiently. Becky bent down to pick up the satchel, and offered it to him.

'Open it.'

Quickly but calmly, Becky undid the straps and held the satchel open so he could see inside it. It contained only two books, nothing else.

'Come on, come on!' he ordered irritably. 'Give them to me so I can look at them properly.'

Once he had the books in his hands, he studied them carefully, slowly leafing through them one at a time. Then he slapped them together and almost threw them back at Becky. For a few moments he continued to contemplate her coldly in silence.

'*Pas op!*'* he warned finally, wagging his finger in front of her nose. 'If you do anything wrong we'll catch you.'

* *Watch out!*

55

He turned on his heels and began walking away slowly, followed an instant later by his companion who, on catching him up, muttered something that made them both laugh.

The unpleasant roughness of their humour shook Candy out of her stupor. 'The swine! . . . The filthy bastards! I could . . .' She swallowed violently. There wasn't anything she could think of doing to them right then that could satisfy her furious hatred.

With a faint grin on her face, Becky was watching the policemen's slow progress across the park. Once she was sure they had gone, she snapped her heels together smartly and bowed mockingly in the direction they had taken. 'Yes my baas, please my baas, thank you my baas – and kick your stupid arse baas,' she finished, giggling.

Candy averted her eyes as Becky sat down beside her again. She was beginning to take stock of what had happened, and her anger was rapidly cooling into fear. The policeman's warning had been directed at them both, she knew that. She had done nothing wrong and yet she had been made to feel an outlaw, vulnerable and exposed in a public place, convinced that everyone's attention had been drawn to her and Becky and that it was hostile. In the sudden grip of panic she wanted to get up and run away.

And then she realized that this was exactly what the policemen had hoped for – to make her feel humiliated and afraid. A new angry stubbornness sprouted up from the core of her fear. She would not be intimidated. The policemen had no right to try and force their Nazi attitudes on her own sense of right and wrong.

Becky meanwhile must have been aware of a little of what she was thinking and drawn her own conclusions from Candy's continuing silence, for she stood up.

'I must go,' she said. 'Here, these books. You can keep them. They'll help you to learn Zulu probably better than I could.' Forcing a smile, she held out the books to Candy.

Candy burned with shame. God, Becky was the one who had actually been humiliated, and here she was, so obsessed with her own reactions that she hadn't spared a single thought for Becky's feelings. Impulsively, she reached out and grabbed Becky's arm.

'Please . . . Don't go,' she said.

'I don't know . . .' Becky shrugged, her expression still closed, proudly indifferent. But after a moment, she sat down slowly.

Candy looked at the cover of one of the two books. The title was in Zulu. She read it out aloud.

'What does it mean?' she asked, happy to find Becky smiling at her suddenly.

'The way you pronounced it, it means something very rude.'

'Really?' Candy laughed. 'Tell me what I said.'

However, Becky shook her head. 'I think maybe you need to learn Zulu from a teacher after all,' she decided. 'Otherwise I can see you getting into a lot of trouble.'

'Well then, when can we start? I was wondering if you would be free to come to my house tomorrow afternoon?'

Becky seemed to take a long time over making up her mind. 'Okay,' she said finally. 'You'd better take those books home with you anyway, so you can have a look at them before the lesson.'

Candy glanced at the first page of the book she had opened. 'I don't think it will help much,' she admitted. 'I can't make any sense of it.'

'Neither could the policeman.'

Their eyes met; and then they both burst out laughing.

'Hey, did you notice he was holding that book upside down when he was looking through it?' Becky said. 'It's lucky for me he couldn't understand it because there's a subversive character in one of the stories.'

'You're not serious?'

Becky nodded. 'It's the truth. There's this zebra, you see, with black and white stripes sharing the same skin.'

She grabbed the book and jumped up, puffing out her chest and pulling an imaginary cap down over her eyes. 'Stand up *jong*,* when I speak to you,' she snarled.

Candy stared at her in surprise.

'Come on, come on! . . .' Becky made as if to hit her.

A brief grin spread over Candy's face. Rising hurriedly to her feet, she assumed an attitude of humble contrition. She was finally beginning to understand and to appreciate Becky's humour. A sense of the ridiculous helped Becky to remain human under an inhuman system; seeing the funny side in her own suffering was both her salvation and her strength.

And despite their power, the policemen were ridiculous. Candy could see that now as Becky stood there mimicking them, with her arms folded and looking down her nose in a silently contemptuous manner.

Trying not to laugh, Candy said, ''Scuse me baas. I didn't do nothing baas.'

Becky nodded grimly. 'You think so, hey? You blerry *bliksem*.† See this book here? What you think you're doing with communist literature, hey? You think I'm stupid. You think I don't know this zebra in here is banned under the Immorality Act?'

'But baas, 'scuse me baas, that zebra's stripes are Separate Development, baas, They grow separate, baas – "Apart", in different areas of the zebra's "heid", baas. They don't cross the Colour Bar, baas. 'Scuse me baas.'

'You cheeky blerry commie. You're under arrest.'

'No baas . . . Please baas . . . Why baas? I didn't do nothing baas.'

'You're under arrest for asking why you're under arrest.'

Candy's control gave way. She doubled up, clutching at

* *boy*   † *scoundrel*

her stomach. Becky collapsed against her, throwing her arm round Candy's shoulder for support.

'Did you see . . .' Becky gasped, 'the way his nose was twitching like a dog's, sniffing for suspect smells between the pages.'

'And what about the other one, with that ludicrous moustache? . . . I bet he files his teeth on it.'

'If he has any. You couldn't see, his lips were pulled in so tight.'

'You know, when he . . .' Candy broke off. Simultaneously, they had become aware of a young white couple walking towards them.

Becky dropped her arm from Candy's shoulder and they automatically moved a little apart from each other. For all their laughter at the policemen, they had learned a lesson about the danger of being too friendly in public.

They parted soon after that. Candy only remembered when Becky had gone, that she had forgotten to give her the train and bus fares for the following day. She could have kicked herself, feeling certain Becky would have a struggle scratching together enough money for the journey.

'Never mind, I'll make it up to her later,' she consoled herself as she joined the bus queue at the terminus. Without consciously thinking about it, she knew she meant the words as a promise involving a lot more than mere compensation for the cost of Becky's fares.

The bus was full. But being near the front of the queue, Candy had managed to get a window seat upstairs, which helped. She hated buses: the stale, sweaty smell of humanity, the unavoidable physical contact with complete strangers. She didn't know how Becky managed to survive the over-crowded Soweto trains.

'In rush hours you can't move – or breathe,' Becky had told her, grinning. 'You could be stabbed to death and you wouldn't have enough air inside you to scream, and nobody would know you were dead until everyone started getting out at the station and you fell over. It's the truth.'

'God!' Candy's earlier anger boiled up inside her. And to think that on top of everything else, Becky had to pay for her own schooling!

Candy knew Becky didn't mean to, but she made her feel so guilty. Guilty for being white. But what could she do? How could she help Becky materially, without incurring a need for gratitude and thus spoiling the sense of equality on which their friendship was founded? Suddenly, it just didn't seem possible that she and Becky would be able to continue relating as equals when everything between them was so unequal.

She glanced at the man in front of her who had turned his head to look through the window. His eyes were pale blue, hard and staring. Candy's heart contracted a little.

She had hated the policeman, she had laughed at him, but he had succeeded in making her nervous. There was no way she could deny that to herself. She looked round the bus at the sea of blank white faces surrounding her, feeling threatened suddenly, and defensive; as if she was an alien hiding among them in disguise. At the same time she found herself despising all of them for the smugness in which they were sitting there by right.

She closed her eyes and leaned against the window to get away from the fat woman next to her who was taking up more than half the seat. She sensed one of her depressions building up. Sometimes, there really didn't seem to be any positive purpose to life at all. It had all been so much easier as a child believing in fairyland, where goodness could be counted on to win hands down in the end, and justice was a quality meted out in strict accordance to the rules.

In reality there didn't appear to be any rules, at least not any that didn't require an act of faith to believe in. That was where God was supposed to come in. Only she had stopped believing in the omnipotent father figure of her Sunday school days. It seemed the height of male chauvinist thinking to visualize God as a He in the first place. Why not a She? Or even more sensibly an It? However, a rational, loving, all-powerful, spiritual intelligence, in whatever image you clothed it, still left the same questions unanswered. It was too easy and unconvincing a way out to say that the Beckys of this world had to suffer in order to store up privileges in Heaven.

The strongest steel has to come through the fire.

Who had first quoted that to her? Oh yes, of course, Uncle Jack. She smiled spontaneously at the memory; and then opened her eyes and glanced round nervously, afraid that somebody might have been watching her and would think she was mad.

Why was it, she wondered, that her favourite uncle always sprang to mind when she was feeling troubled? She supposed it was because she had always felt so close to him, and had always been able to talk to him about anything at all – even things she would have been embarrassed to discuss with her parents.

She hadn't thought of Uncle Jack for some time, but now she found herself wishing fervently that she could talk to him about Becky. However, he was thousands of miles away in London, where he had been living for the past six years.

. . . *The strongest steel has to come through the fire.*

Yes, at least that made more sense than treasures in heaven. Nevertheless, it still couldn't help justify Becky's lot in life. If Becky's suffering enabled her to become stronger, what good was it ultimately if it couldn't also actually improve her position? Except in a personal sense – she was forgetting that. She remembered the way Becky had laughed at the policemen, and how much she had admired her ability to do it. Perhaps in all this there was one positive answer to all the negative whys and wherefores of existence: the individual human spirit obviously had the potential strength to withstand any political or social force aimed at suppressing it.

The bus swerved suddenly, braking. Candy flung out her arm to stop herself falling against the seat in front. A green Putco bus roared by, going in the opposite direction. Candy was aware of a blur of black faces mirroring surprise, fear, shock, as the two buses passed within mere inches of each other.

'Savages!' the woman beside her exclaimed furiously, grabbing back her shopping which had slithered off her lap on to Candy. 'Did you see how fast he was going? He nearly killed us all. They've got no road sense – or respect, those Bantu bus drivers. They should be shot, the lot of them. They're just a menace to everybody else . . . A menace, that's what they are.'

She looked at Candy as if expecting her to agree. When Candy remained silent, the woman settled herself back irritably in her seat. 'Savages!' she muttered again.

Candy glanced past her at the other passengers. A few of them seemed shocked, but mostly they looked angry. Several voices were raised in audible and indignant denunciation of black drivers. However, as the bus picked up speed once more, newspapers were re-opened, normal conversations resumed, and heads began nodding back to sleep.

God! Candy thought. *We are all fast asleep, complacently caught up in a dream world behind our locked doors of white privilege.*

But I can't go on like this, she realized suddenly. *Not any longer.* Meeting Becky had jolted her a fraction awake, and now she couldn't fall back into the same, self-satisfied sleep, even if she wanted to. The knowledge frightened her, and yet at the same time, she felt it as a strengthening of her resolve. She would not be put off by her parents' nervousness and the policeman's threatening *Pas op!* She already liked Becky tremendously, and she knew that was what she had to draw on, in facing up to whatever might lie ahead.

3

Candy swallowed her tea without tasting it. She wasn't thirsty, she had had a second cup simply to stop herself fidgeting nervously while waiting for Becky to arrive. It was her mother who was making her nervous.

Her mother had been in a feverish flap all morning, spreading tension through the household like a highly contagious, supersonic sneeze. Tom had been the first casualty, breaking out into a rare bad temper after being continually chivvied to have the lunch ready earlier than usual.

'What's wrong with the madam today?' he complained crossly to Candy at one point. 'What she think I am? A *shongololo** with *maningi*† hands and feet? Look at the time already. I can't make the oven go faster.'

'No, you can't,' Candy agreed sympathetically. She couldn't very well tell him that her mother was trying to hurry him up to have him safely out of the way before Becky arrived.

However, he obviously knew a guest was expected because he said, 'It's nonsense, this. Why the madam must make a cake this morning while I'm trying to cook? Now all the flour is gone, so what must I do? Who's coming anyway? The Queen of Engaland?'

Candy smiled, knowing how much he hated her mother using 'his' kitchen while he was there. But she felt as irritated as he was by her mother's behaviour which suggested they must be expecting a person of great public importance, not a mere schoolgirl.

Candy's father, wisely, had taken himself out of the line of fire very early, disappearing into the garden straight after

*   *millipede*   † *many*

breakfast and remaining hidden among his rose-bushes until lunchtime. And to Candy's relief, Colin had spent most of the morning in bed, playing his limited collection of pop records over and over again at top volume. Normally, his total disregard for the sensitivity of everyone else's eardrums would have driven Candy to distraction. But on this particular Sunday she was only thankful that he was not around to add further to her mother's panic.

Candy had tried very hard to keep well clear of the turbulence that seemed to surround all her mother's activities. However, she hadn't been able to help noticing how often her mother was to be found hovering near a suitable window, darting odd, anxious glances in the direction of the next-door-neighbours' garden, as if she was hoping to see them all emerge from their house and drive away for the afternoon. It had set Candy's own nerves on edge, bringing to mind the incident with the two constables in the park. She kept remembering cases she had heard of or read about, in which the defendants had claimed they had been harassed by the police, interrogated and even imprisoned, for no other reason than that they had lived their private lives in bold defiance of the social regulations of apartheid. She had always tended to discount such cases; people weren't arrested unless they were actively engaged in political subversion. Now she was no longer so sure.

In the end, however, a sense of loyalty to her friendship with Becky prevailed, and her stubborn streak came to the fore. She had made up her mind that she was not going to be intimidated, or influenced by other people's fear. She recognized the feeling she had had when as a child she believed she had been wrongly punished for something. But there was a difference: then the feeling had been part of the frustration of helpless dependence, whereas now it reinforced her awareness of her own independence and strength. And it enabled her to feel more tolerant, suddenly, of her mother's state of panic. Putting down her empty tea cup, she grinned with confident indulgence at her mother's back.

'It's still there, is it – their car?' she teased.

Her mother swung round and moved away from the veranda railings.

'What car, dear? I was just admiring the way Dad's designed the border of flowers along the side fence. I think you're absolutely right, Ron. We probably don't need a hedge there after all. In a year or two, when the shrubs have thickened out a little, that side of the garden is going to be quite cosy and private. More tea, anyone? What about you, Ron?'

There was an affirmative grunt, followed by a rustling, and Candy's father's hand appeared round the side of his Sunday newspaper, holding out a cup which his wife obligingly filled.

Candy watched this little ritual of her parents with amusement, although some months back she had begun to resent her father's habit of hiding himself behind a newspaper at breakfast and tea times, and taking it for granted that her mother would wait on him.

'You shouldn't spoil him like that,' she had angrily scolded her mother. 'Don't you care about women's liberation? You ought to make him get up and help himself. At least he would have to show his face then. And who knows, it might even encourage him to talk to you occasionally, instead of merely grunting.'

'Don't be silly, dear, I don't *really* spoil him at all.' Her mother had hotly defended herself. 'And anyway, what if I did? He spoils me in lots of little ways too.'

'Oh yes? Like what?'

'Oh . . . in lots of little ways you can't possibly be expected to know about. You're forgetting he brings me coffee in bed every morning, for instance, and has done ever since we got married.'

Candy had forgotten that.

'Anyway,' her mother had continued, 'I don't mind him reading his newspaper, so why should you? He doesn't mind my chatter, and I don't mind his reading – we communicate perfectly well. He's the dearest man really, and I wouldn't have him any different, so there.'

The fierce tenderness in her voice had taken Candy by surprise. Ever since then she had viewed her parents' relationship in a slightly different light, with a greater appreciation of their comfortable bond of mutual need and affection, which had obviously strengthened over the years despite the differences and difficulties between them to which Candy had been sensitive from an early age.

'Would *you* like another cup, dear?' her mother was saying. 'There's probably just about enough left in the pot.'

Candy shook her head. She didn't really like tea at the best of times and her second cup, straight after her roast meal, had left her feeling uncomfortably full. Not that she had eaten so much, but her stomach hadn't been feeling very settled to begin with.

'Well, I'll take the tray through to the kitchen then, and see if Tom has finished the washing-up yet. I don't know why he's being so slow today, and so grumpy. You'd think he'd be only too glad to get away early for once on his afternoon off.'

'Poor Tom,' Candy thought. She sighed and picked up the Sunday newspaper supplement.

But she was too restless to read so she went and sat in the sunshine on the veranda steps and stared out over the garden. She imagined Becky admiring the large, lush lawn, the blaze of colours in the flower beds, the carefully-shaped shrubberies, and herself trying to excuse it all by saying, 'Well, you see, my dad's a very good gardener.'

Her mother and Colin were talking in the passage. A few moments later they both came out on to the veranda.

'I'll be off then,' Colin said.

'Where are you going, dear?'

'Just out. I might drop in on Dave.' Candy sensed Colin looking at her before he added, 'You don't think I'm going to stick around with half of Soweto coming to tea, do you?'

'Don't be so silly,' her mother told him. 'Candy has only got one black friend coming, after all, and we aren't breaking any law by having her here.'

Candy noticed the uncertainty in her mother's voice, and so, obviously, did Colin. He laughed.

'Don't worry, Ma,' he said. 'I'll consider passing you the odd peanut through the prison bars.'

As he went past Candy on the steps he ran his fingers roughly across the top of her hair. 'Better watch it,' he called back over his shoulder. 'It feels like it's starting to go crinkly already.'

Candy looked at her mother, who shrugged helplessly and then looked at Candy's father. 'I wish you would make him wear his crash helmet, Ron. He just won't listen to me about it.'

Candy's father grunted and muttered something inaudible. A few seconds later, Colin roared past on his motorcycle, skidded through the gateway and streaked off up the road out of sight.

Candy's father was instantly on his feet, furiously flapping his newspaper at the wispy trails of exhaust fumes floating slowly across the veranda.

'The insolent little bugger. Just wait till I get my hands on him. I don't know how many times I've told him not to start that damn monstrosity until he's out in the street. If I had my way, I'd ban the stinking lot of them from the roads. They shouldn't be allowed to go around making such a racket and destroying everyone else's peace and quiet.'

Candy's mother fingered her fresh hair-do nervously. 'I

wish he wouldn't go so fast,' she complained. 'I'm so scared he'll have an accident on it one of these days.'

'It'd teach him a lesson if he did come off the damn thing, the way he rides it.'

'Hear! Hear!' Candy agreed softly as her mother gave her father a horrified look.

'You mustn't talk like that, Ron. Tempting fate. It's awful.'

'Well . . . you know what I mean . . . Anyway, I'd better go and finish off that pruning. There's not much time left. I told Bill we'd be there at four.'

'Today? But it's not today we're meant to be going? I thought the arrangement was . . .'

'Of course it's today. Dammit, girlie, I told you, Bill wants me to help plant those saplings. And we're meant to be staying on for supper, remember?'

'But I can't possibly go today. I'm sure you said it was next week. I can't go today . . . not now.'

There was a short, tense silence. Candy knew what was coming. She stood up impatiently.

'I mean, how can I?' her mother went on in an agitated tone. 'Not with this . . . this friend of Candy's coming. I must be here, it would be . . .'

'Why?' Candy cut in irritably. 'Why must you be here because I've got a friend coming? Don't you think I'm old enough to . . .'

'That's not the point, dear. This isn't a normal sit . . .'

'Isn't normal?' Candy almost shouted. 'Good God Almighty! . . . What's so abnormal about . . .'

'That's enough, do you hear?' her father rounded on her fiercely. 'I've had a bellyful of all this. You've already caused enough trouble for one day. You just hold your tongue and leave your mother and me to sort this out. It's got nothing to do with you.'

Candy couldn't have agreed with him less, but she didn't

dare argue the point. He seemed cross enough as it was, and when he really lost his temper he frightened her.

'Now Susan,' he went on, turning back to his wife. 'You know we can't let Bill and June down. Those saplings have to be planted today, so we ought to leave by quarter to four at the latest. No . . . let me finish, will you. I can't see any reason why you have to be here. In fact, it will probably be better if you aren't. You'll only work yourself up into a worse state unnecessarily.'

That was a fatal thing to say. 'What exactly do you mean by that?' his wife demanded, squaring up to him angrily. 'What state do you think I'm in, I'd like to know?'

'Now there's going to be fireworks,' Candy thought despairingly. It was all she needed with Becky due to arrive in about fifteen minutes. She had a sudden urge to giggle. All this fuss and bother over Becky's visit was becoming farcical. Except that it wasn't really in the slightest bit funny.

However, to her relief, her father decided to back down for some reason. With a placating smile, he said in an altogether different tone of voice, 'Please don't get upset, girlie. I wasn't referring to any particular state. All I was trying to say was that I just don't want you worrying yourself unnecessarily. Candy is perfectly capable of looking after this . . . this visitor of hers on her own, in a sensible manner. And you know how disappointed Bill and June will be if we let them down now, at the last moment.'

That seemed to satisfy Candy's mother, at least sufficiently to douse the blazing anger in her eyes into a smouldering stubbornness, reminding Candy a little uncomfortably of herself in an argument.

'There's no need to let them down, Ron. You go on ahead of me and do what you have to do in the garden for Bill, and I'll come over later in time for dinner.'

'But that's ridiculous. It means I'll have to come back and fetch you.'

'Of course it doesn't. I'll come over in my own car.'

'But you can't, girlie. You know the battery is flat.'

Candy's mother shrugged. 'I'll start it somehow. If need be, Candy can give me a push down the drive.'

'This is just too damned ridiculous,' Candy's father said, starting to get angry all over again.

Candy almost managed to feel sorry for him then, knowing that what was really bothering him was the prospect of having to go out visiting on his own. Beneath his gruffness, she had recently realized, he was basically rather shy and he tended to rely on her mother's talkativeness as his social shield.

'I'll ring June and tell her I'll be over later,' her mother said firmly. 'Now let's not go on about this any more, Ron. I feel I must stay, and that's that,' and she smiled at him confidently.

'You are . . .' he began. Then he threw up his arms in exasperation and stamped off down the steps into the garden.

Candy frowned at her mother, but she had turned her back and was bending down to pick up the newspaper her husband had flung on the floor earlier.

'I haven't really had a chance to look at it properly today,' her mother remarked aloud to herself. 'Perhaps I'll put my feet up now for a few minutes.'

However, she had barely settled herself comfortably when the kitchen yard door slammed and footsteps crunched closer round the side of the house. Candy's mother immediately stood up and took off her spectacles.

'Ah, there goes Tom now, at last,' she said.

Candy raised her eyes in time to see him disappearing down the driveway, dressed in his usual Sunday best of flannel trousers, checked sports jacket and matching felt hat, tilted at an angle over one ear. He was obviously still in a bad mood because he didn't turn and doff his hat towards the veranda as he normally would have done.

'Well, now that he's gone I'll go and get the tray ready for your visitor's tea,' her mother said brightly. 'What time do you think you'll be wanting it, dear?'

'I've no idea. What does it matter? I can do it myself when we're ready for it.' Seeing Tom had made Candy suddenly suspicious of her mother's motive.

'Well, I'll just get the tray ready anyway.'

'Why? So you can make sure your best crockery isn't used? What are you going to do – put out Tom's cup for Becky?' The dart went home. She saw the shocked hurt in her mother's eyes, and she immediately regretted her hasty judgement.

For a moment, neither of them spoke. Then Candy said, 'I'm sorry Mum. It's just that . . .'

It's all right, dear.' Her mother smiled thinly. 'We're all a bit edgy today.'

'*What's the use*,' Candy thought. She checked her watch and was relieved to find it was time to go and meet Becky off the bus. Knowing her mother would worry about the neighbours seeing her and Becky walking to the house together, she hoped her mother wouldn't ask her where she was going. However, she did.

'Just to the bottom of the road,' Candy told her brusquely, and left the veranda before her mother could utter more than a surprised and anxious-sounding 'Oh'.

*   *   *

Becky licked her fingers appreciatively. 'That was very good,' she declared. 'Who baked the cake? You?'

Candy shook her head. 'My mother did. Have another piece.' She cut a large slice and manoeuvred it on to Becky's plate.

'Your mother's a very good cook.'

'Yes . . .' Candy hesitated. Was Becky making fun of her? She must know that Candy's mother would almost certainly have a black servant to do most of the cooking. 'My mother's good at baking, anyway,' Candy muttered.

71

Becky giggled. 'You shouldn't have given me such a big second piece. Your mother will think I'm very greedy.'

'Of course she won't. She'll feel complimented. After all, she made the cake specially for our tea.' Candy was thankful she could at least say that much truthfully.

There was a short silence, then Becky asked abruptly, 'Your mother didn't mind me coming?'

'Good grief! No. Why should she?'

But Candy didn't dare raise her face as Becky said, 'Well . . . you know . . .'

After a brief pause, Becky went on gaily, 'Hey, what a lot of books you've got.' Getting up off the bed, she went across to the shelves lining the opposite wall.

Candy watched her, intrigued by the way she carefully wiped her hands on her dress before stretching up to touch the nearest books slowly, almost reverently, as if they were rare icons inspiring her awe.

'I love books,' she said over her shoulder.

'Help yourself. Borrow as many as you like.'

'I wouldn't know where to begin.' However, almost immediately Becky selected a book and held it up for Candy to see. 'Shakespeare. You've got the complete works. I'm trying to collect all his plays and learn them off by heart. So far I've only managed to get *The Tempest* and *Hamlet*. Do you like *Hamlet*?'

Candy remembered her English essay. 'I think there's quite a lot in it,' she said. 'And you? Do you like *Hamlet*?'

But Becky wasn't listening. She had opened the book and was reading something, frowning. When she did speak, there was a fierce intensity in her voice.

'I love Shakespeare to my heart. I don't understand all his words, but he writes so big, you know?'

'Yes?' Candy said uncertainly. 'He's very bloody though, isn't he. You trip over corpses on every page. It puts me off.'

Becky shook her head. 'He writes raw. You know, what's

underneath: the weakness and the strength; the struggles, the terrible suffering of the soul. The bad and the good and the payment at the end after so much agony. And then sometimes he can be so funny and with feeling. I like that.'

Candy stared at her, a little stunned by the unexpected glimpse into the apparently passionate depths of Becky's mind. It made her feel suddenly superficial and frivolous by comparison, full of doubt about her own capacity for experiencing such intensity. Acting on impulse, she crossed the room and took the book from Becky's hands. Finding a pen, she scribbled hastily on the flyleaf.

'*To Becky, from Friendship for Learning.*' Becky read it through twice aloud and then looked up, surprised.

'Now you can learn all the plays off by heart at your leisure,' Candy told her.

'But . . .'

'No buts. I don't use the book, honestly. I've hardly ever even opened it – look at the dust. You'll make far better use of it than I do.' Nothing would have pleased Candy more right then than to have been able to give Becky all the rest of her books as well, for the same reason.

As Becky remained uncertain, Candy urged, 'Please take it. I'll be very hurt if you don't.'

Slowly, Becky smiled. 'Okay then. If you're sure. Thank you very much. It's a beautiful book.' She ran her fingers over the cover as if she was stroking something alive. 'I'll treasure it always.'

Candy turned away, embarrassed but also pleased. She had found one practical way in which she could help Becky. She could give her books. It should be easier than trying to give her money.

Becky didn't follow her back to the bed. Instead, she went to the window and stood looking out at the garden. Candy wondered uneasily what she was thinking. She was surprised when Becky suddenly laughed.

'Aren't you worried about that big tree growing so near your window?'

'Why? You mean in case it falls on the house?'

'No, in case it has a Special Branch.' As Candy looked blank, Becky explained, 'You know how much Special Branch *bobbejaans* like to climb up trees to spy into people's bedrooms.'

'Oh yes.' Candy smiled, remembering a well-publicised Immorality case some years back where a security policeman had climbed a tree overlooking the bedroom of a house in a white suburb to catch the unfortunate couple in the act. 'I'd better remember to draw my curtains in future, hadn't I?'

'For sure.'

'Actually,' Candy said, 'I forgot to mention that we do have one Copper about the place.'

'Copper? What's that?'

'It's slang for a policeman.' She tried to keep a straight face, but it was difficult with the way Becky was looking at her. 'It's the truth,' she teased. 'We really do have a Copper. He's a bit of a pig too, like all coppers. It's okay though, he doesn't shoot pellets, he just eats them.'

Becky was astonished. 'You keep a pig in the garden?'

Candy nodded. 'But he's only a guinea pig.'

'Ah.' Becky grinned. 'A guinea pig, hey! I don't know much about them. The only pigs I know about are Rand pigs.'

'Would you like to meet our Copper then?'

'No. They bite, don't they?'

'Don't all coppers?' Candy said sardonically.

'I bit a policeman once, you know.'

'You didn't?'

Becky giggled. 'You know what we call policemen? *Amakgathas.*'

'What's that mean?'

'It's very rude.'

'Tell me.'

'Arseholes.'

Candy laughed, feeling her nervousness and anxiety dissipating. As Becky sat down on the bed beside her, she handed her a pillow, and they both leaned back, resting comfortably against the wall.

'You didn't really bite a policeman, did you?'

'I did too. It's the truth. I was only maybe four or five then. He was a "blackjack" – you know, the municipal policemen who carry out the raids on houses in the early hours of the morning to catch people who aren't registered on the house permits. You know about house permits?'

Candy shook her head apologetically.

'Well, you know you can't own a house outright in Soweto?'

Candy nodded, too ashamed to admit ignorance.

'And to get a permit to lease a house, you have to satisfy certain regulations – like, if you're a woman, you just can't get one at all . . . I know,' she said, shrugging at Candy's suddenly angry expression. 'But what can you do? . . . Anyway, if you can get a permit, you have to register all your dependants on it. And these blackjacks – we call them that because they're dressed all in black, I suppose so you can't see them coming in the dark – they try to catch people who aren't on the permit. We hate them like anything. They make you so scared, especially when you're very small.' She shivered, reliving her fear in memory.

'So you bit one?' Candy prompted, finally beginning to believe in the likelihood of it.

'Hard too, like anything.' Becky grinned proudly. 'They broke into our house very early one morning when we were all asleep. They bang on the door and then they just kick it in if you don't open it quickly – they don't care. I woke up and there was a lot of shouting and these evil eyes flashing – they carry torches, you see. And I thought the devil had sent

75

his spirits to get me because my mother had told me he would if I was naughty, and I had been naughty that day. So I screamed like anything and ran fast like a rabbit out the back door and across the yard to the lavatory. I thought I'd be safe there because demons don't have to go . . . you know . . . like people, so they wouldn't think to look for me there. But to be extra safe, I crawled behind the . . . what's it called again? You know, the part you sit on?'

'The bowl?'

'That's right. So I squeezed in behind that as far as I could, and then I started praying to God to forgive me for being naughty, and to keep the demons away from me. Only I was shaking so hard I could only stutter, and I was afraid God wouldn't be able to understand what I was trying to say, or that He was asleep . . . Well, He must have been,' she went on wryly, 'because next moment the door opened and this bright, evil eye glared in. Ooohh! . . .' She started suddenly, clutching at her breast, and despite herself, Candy jumped nervously.

They both laughed. 'I was frightened like anything, I can tell you,' Becky said, shaking her head. 'But you know why the blackjack had come there?'

Candy guessed and started laughing again.

'It wasn't so funny at the time, I can tell you,' Becky said.

'No, I'm sure it wasn't. What did you do?'

'Well, I was like this, see . . .' Becky crouched down on the bed. 'And it was very dark – he'd put his torch in his pocket to take down his trousers. And all I could make out was this heavy shape coming down on top of me. I still thought it was an evil spirit come to get me. Suddenly, I remembered somebody telling me that if you met the devil or any of his messengers, you mustn't let them get close enough to touch you because they were so hot from living in hell you'd straightaway burn up. The only thing to do if they cornered you was to bite them. So that's what I did,' she confessed with a roguish smile. 'I bit his arse.'

The way she said it, with such triumph, gnashing her teeth in demonstration, sent Candy into hysterics. In a way, it was a tremendous relief to be able to laugh at something which, as a description of law enforcement in Soweto, was rather horrific.

'You haven't heard the funniest part yet,' Becky managed to splutter finally, supporting herself weakly against Candy's shoulder. 'The blackjack thought *I* was an evil spirit . . . It's the truth. My mother told me he came running into the house, tripping over his trousers and shouting something about a *spook*.* He made the other blackjacks so scared they all rushed away and didn't come back. Since that time they've never been back, which is lucky because now my other uncle and aunt are living . . .' She broke off, drawing her breath in sharply as if she was suddenly afraid she had said too much.

'What about your other uncle and aunt?'

Becky shrugged. 'Nothing.'

Candy didn't press her further, but she couldn't help feeling hurt that Becky obviously didn't trust her enough to go on.

They were both silent for a moment, then Becky brightened and gave Candy a playful push.

'Hey,' she said, 'you know there's still some people who won't use our lavatory when they come to visit us. Word got round that it's bewitched, you see.'

'BeBeckied, you mean.' Candy laughed when Becky did. She was about to say more when Becky pulled away from her and sat up straight.

'I've just come to get the tea tray.'

Candy's mother was standing in the doorway, looking embarrassed.

'Oh . . . hallo, Mum,' Candy said. Suddenly conscious of

* *ghost*

77

the noise she and Becky must have been making, she explained, 'Becky has just been telling me how she once bit a policeman,' and then realized her mistake as she saw her mother's face close up.

'It was during a police raid on her house in Soweto,' Candy rushed on recklessly, unable to stop herself now that she had started. 'Becky was very young at the time and she thought the policeman was an evil spirit come to get her.'

'Oh.' Her mother smiled stiffly. 'Have you finished with the tray, dear?'

'Yes . . . we have.'

Candy avoided looking at Becky, but she heard her say, 'Thank you very much for the cake. It was very delicious.'

'Oh, not at all. I'm glad you liked it.'

Candy's mother picked up the tray and turned away. She was almost at the door when she stopped and smiled over her shoulder at a point somewhere above Candy's and Becky's heads.

'I'm going to make myself another cup of tea,' she said. 'Perhaps you girls might like a fresh pot?'

Candy glanced at Becky who shook her head – the first movement she had made since Candy's mother had come into the room.

'Not for me, thank you,' she said. 'I have to go home soon. But thank you very much for the tea.'

'Not at all,' and Candy's mother hurried out.

Becky stood up. 'I'd better go now,' she said.

'Do you have to?' Candy was aware that the atmosphere had changed, and she was afraid that Becky was leaving because she felt unwelcome.

'I told my mother I would be home before it's dark, and Soweto is very far, you know.'

'I know,' Candy said. At that moment, the distance between her and Becky seemed just as far. 'Well . . . we didn't manage to get round to the lesson.'

78

'You still want to learn Zulu?'

'Of course. I was hoping you would be able to come every Sunday afternoon to teach me. Could you manage that, do you think?'

'Okay,' said Becky, grinning suddenly. 'I can manage that, if that's what you want. But next Sunday we'd better start the lesson straightaway because you know what we're like. We talk too much.'

Candy laughed, feeling happier again. 'I did learn something today though. I now know what to call a policeman.'

Becky's grin widened. 'I wouldn't use that word,' she warned, 'unless you can run faster than a rabbit.'

Before they left for the bus stop, Candy bullied Becky into accepting the money for her fares. With some difficulty, she also managed to make her take enough money for the following Sunday as well.

'It's only fair,' Candy argued, 'seeing as you're the one who will always have to do the travelling.'

Becky finally shrugged, and allowed Candy to push the money into her pocket. She couldn't really afford to be too proud, as Candy knew only too well.

They had been walking for a little while when Becky said, 'You know, I don't think your mother found it very funny about the blackjack.'

Candy blushed. 'I'm sorry,' she said. 'Perhaps I shouldn't have mentioned it. I'm sorry if I embarrassed you.'

'Oh, that's okay. I don't mind. But I think your mother was embarrassed.'

Candy blushed deeper. 'Don't worry about her,' she said quickly. 'She thinks as much of policemen as I do. That's why I told her. But she's very shy really, that's all.'

'Me too,' said Becky, giggling. After a moment, she added, 'I like her. I think she's very nice.'

'I'm glad. I'm sure she likes you too,' Candy mumbled, and was thankful to find they had reached the main road and were in sight of Becky's bus stop, and so she didn't have to say any more.

Three African women were already standing there. Seeing them, the two girls slowed down and turned aside. Without consciously realizing it, they chose to take their farewell of each other at a neutral point, almost exactly halfway between the two bus stops – the one reserved exclusively for whites, and the other, lower down the road, for blacks.

'You needn't wait,' Becky said.

'Of course I will.'

However, they had little to say to each other now that they were surrounded by strangers, and they were both obviously relieved when Becky's bus finally appeared through the traffic.

Candy waited to make sure that Becky got on the bus and then waved to her as it went past. She was aware of the other faces in the bus staring at her, surprised to see a young white girl waving so energetically at a bus full of Africans. Feeling suddenly vulnerable, she glanced round to see if anyone was staring. Then angry with herself for caring, she turned and began to walk home slowly.

*　　*　　*

It was after midnight when Candy heard her parents' cars come up the drive. She switched on the bedside lamp and sat up. It was pointless to go on trying to get to sleep; she was as wide awake as ever.

Perhaps if she took a couple of aspirin? . . . But no, she didn't have a headache – there wasn't anything physically wrong with her at all. She was just feeling restless and depressed.

She glanced round the room. It seemed different somehow; it didn't *feel* the same. It was no longer a sanctuary, her place of safety, where she could shut herself away from the world when something was bothering her, and find a sense of security among her most personal possessions.

Wherever she looked she saw Becky: standing at the bookshelves; staring out of the window; sitting beside her on the bed, laughing.

He writes so raw . . . the terrible suffering . . . so much agony . . . weakness and strength . . . and then . . . so funny and with feeling. I like that.

Candy shook her head. She really was some girl, was Becky. *So that's what I did, I bit his arse.*

Candy had to smile. She realized suddenly that Becky made her laugh more than anyone else she knew. She seemed to have a vitality and spontaneity that sparked off Candy when they were together.

And yet, as soon as she had gone, Candy had started to feel out of sorts with herself. She couldn't settle down to anything, although she didn't know if she felt angry or sad or what, which made it even worse.

She got out of bed and went to the door. She could hear her parents talking and laughing in the lounge. They had obviously had a few drinks and were in a good humour. The sound of their merriment drew her like a beacon. Perhaps their company would cheer her up.

However, when she reached the lounge door, she stopped, uncertain. Maybe she was intruding on their privacy; maybe they were feeling amorous and wanted to be alone. She couldn't imagine it, but she supposed they still did make love occasionally.

Then she heard her mother giggle and say, 'I'll go and make us some coffee. You'd better have yours black,' and taking this as her cue, opened the door.

Her parents were standing together in front of the fireplace. They looked round startled, then her mother smiled.

'Hallo, dear. What are you doing still up at this time of night?'

'I couldn't sleep. I was wondering if you'd like some coffee?'

'That would be lovely. I was just going to make some myself. You'd better give Dad an extra strong cup,' her mother added.

'Don't be ridiculous,' Candy's father snorted. 'I'm perfectly sober. You're the one who . . .'

'Never! I never drink much, you know that. I only had two small glasses of sherry.'

'And a glass of wine.'

'Well? That's still not much. It's hardly enough to . . .'

Candy left them to their bickering. She felt both amused by, and a little envious of, their unusual frivolity. Her mother, in particular, drank very seldom and then only a little at a time. But one glassful was usually enough to make her rather girlish and giggly, and Candy enjoyed the novelty of seeing her like that. It gave her a glimpse of what her mother might have been like when she was a lot younger. At such times, Candy was also almost able to imagine her mother capable of wild passion. She would never forget the occasion when they had had guests to dinner and her mother, after two glasses of champagne, had got up from the table at Colin's bidding, and given a hilarious impersonation of a striptease artist who was currently featuring in all the newspapers as a result of being charged with indecency. Candy's father had been very embarrassed by his wife's performance – much to everyone else's further amusement.

When Candy had handed out the coffee, she took hers and perched on the edge of a chair, listening to her mother's giggly account of the evening. She tried hard to respond, but her mother must have sensed something of her mood because she stopped suddenly in mid-sentence, and asked, 'Are you all right, dear? Aren't you feeling well?'

Candy shrugged. 'I'm okay. Why?'

'You're looking a little pale.'

'You should be in bed,' Candy's father commented, not unkindly.

'I'm not feeling tired.'

Candy was beginning to realize what she was waiting for – why she had sought out her parents' company in the first place. She wanted to talk to them about Becky; or rather, she wanted them to mention her first so that she could then tell them about Becky's house and her family, and the black-jacks, and the terrible conditions at her school.

However, it became obvious, when her parents started to talk about going to bed, that neither of them was going to refer to Becky's visit that afternoon. It was as though they had intentionally drawn a veil of silence over the subject.

Noticing that her mother was about to get up, Candy asked a little desperately, 'Well, did you like Becky then?'

'Damn!' Candy's father said suddenly, looking around irritably. 'I must have left my glasses in the car. I'd better go and check in case I left them at Bill and June's.'

'You couldn't have done, Ron. I'm sure you had them on when we came into the house.' Candy's mother jumped up. 'Did you look in . . .' she began, but her husband had already left the room. She picked up his empty cup and put it on the tray. 'Thank you for the coffee, dear,' she said over her shoulder. 'It was very welcome.'

'Mum! I asked you a question.'

'Oh, yes . . . I'm sorry, dear. She seems a nice enough girl, as far as one can tell. Pleasant and well-mannered. . . . Now are you sure you're all right, and that you'll be able to sleep? You wouldn't like an aspirin or something?'

Candy shook her head peevishly. 'I presume then that you won't mind her coming every Sunday afternoon to give me Zulu lessons?'

'Now wait a minute. You mustn't put words into my mouth. I haven't had a proper chance to think . . .'

'What's there to think about? You've met Becky and you've seen what she's like, so . . .'

'I've told you before it's not that simple,' her mother said, beginning to get angry herself. 'You have to consider . . .'

'What the neighbours might think,' Candy finished for her.

'No. How many times do I have to tell you? There are a lot of . . .'

'Well, I've already asked her to come next Sunday.' Candy gave her mother a sullen, defiant look. 'I assumed it would be okay now that you know what she's like.'

'You had no right to do . . .' Her mother hiccuped suddenly. The look of surprise on her face would normally have made Candy laugh. As it was, she had to struggle not to smile.

Her mother hiccuped again. 'This is silly,' she said, and started to giggle. 'Coffee always seems to do this to me after sherry. It's rid . . . iculous really.'

'I don't see how I can let Becky down now when I've already asked her to come,' Candy insisted sulkily.

'You should . . . n't have . . .' Her mother patted her chest. 'Oh dear, this is terrible. Anyone would think I was drunk . . . Well, it's too late now to do anything about this Sunday, see . . . ing – excuse me – that you've already arranged it with her. But I'm not sure it will be a good idea for her to come every Sunday. We'll have to see.' She grabbed the tray and started towards the door.

'Now you go and get straight into bed, you hear?' she called sternly from the passage.

Candy met her father coming out of the bathroom. She refused to look at him, but as they passed each other, he unexpectedly stretched out and ruffled her hair. It was something he hadn't done for a long time, and it had a strange effect on her. She suddenly wanted to cry as she went on into her bedroom and closed the door. She didn't know why it was, but on the rare occasions that her father was impulsively demonstrative, he never failed to stir her emotions deeply.

She got into bed and turned out the light, no longer feeling angry, but simply sad in a gentle, resigned sort of way. She was soon asleep.

4

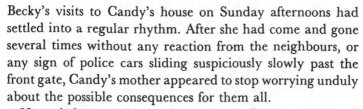

Becky's visits to Candy's house on Sunday afternoons had settled into a regular rhythm. After she had come and gone several times without any reaction from the neighbours, or any sign of police cars sliding suspiciously slowly past the front gate, Candy's mother appeared to stop worrying unduly about the possible consequences for them all.

Nevertheless, as the weeks wore on, Candy was disappointed to find both her parents continuing to show little inclination to get to know Becky directly, or even to discuss her. Candy found her mother's silence on the subject particularly upsetting because she normally took such an avid interest in Candy's friends and social activities. With regard to Becky, however, she went no further than to inquire, with conscientious regularity each week, how the Zulu lessons were progressing. Knowing that these stood as some sort of safeguard in her mother's mind against her fear of overstepping even the spirit, let alone the actual letter of the law of apartheid, Candy felt obliged to protect her from the truth.

'They're coming along slowly,' she would tell her, when in fact they hadn't really started. She and Becky were finding too much else to talk about during their few hours together to feel any sense of urgency in fulfilling Becky's tongue-in-cheek promise of making Candy into a 'First-class Zulu'. In the course of their conversations, Candy was picking up a little Zulu vocabulary. But most of the words Becky mentioned in passing, and laughingly translated for her benefit, were rude references to the numerous forces of oppression in Soweto, which didn't make them very suitable for demonstrating Candy's knowledge of the language.

However, in more important ways, Candy was aware of

learning a lot from Becky every Sunday. She was learning about the actual face of apartheid; a face which she had only known in vague outline before, viewed dimly from too impersonal a distance to have to confront its character or feel the shadows cast by its form. Now Becky was bringing it close-up and showing her its frightening features one by one.

A specially disturbing feature was the complicated system of pass laws – laws which made it obligatory for all Africans from the age of sixteen to carry a pass or reference book with them at all times of the day and night. In the reference book – or 'stinker' as Becky called it – were personal details and a photograph, as well as information relating to the possessor's rights of residence in a certain area, and his or her type and place of employment. Failure to produce a pass instantly on demand by a policeman meant automatic arrest, as did any failure within the pass to comply with the necessary legal specifications.

Before meeting Becky, Candy had known that the pass laws were both an inconvenience and an insult to black people. What she had not realized was the virtual power of life and death they held over every individual African. This was something, however, which Becky soon made her understand all too clearly.

They had been talking about birthdays, and Candy happened to mention how pleased she was that she would be turning sixteen soon.

When Becky didn't say anything, Candy asked her innocently, 'Won't you be glad to be sixteen?'

'You crazy?' Becky answered sharply. 'You think I'm looking forward to having to carry a "stinker" round with me wherever I go for the rest of my life?'

'Oh, yes, of course,' Candy said. 'I'm sorry. I was forgetting about that. Mind you . . . I mean, I know it's not nearly the same or anything, but I'll have to get a Book of Life.'*

* Identity Document

86

Becky gave a hollow laugh. 'You get a Book of Life when you turn sixteen, we get a Book of Death.'

'Really? It's honestly that bad, is it?'

'I can tell you, it's worse.'

'How come?'

Becky shrugged. 'My best friend turned sixteen a little while ago, so she had to get a pass. Right? Well, she should have been okay, no problems. She qualified under Section Ten: she was born in Soweto, her parents' permits were in order. Nothing was wrong. Just one thing – her mother hadn't registered her birth, so she couldn't prove she qualified to stay there. The official who interviewed her wouldn't listen to her. He wouldn't believe her, or her mother, or her father, or anyone. He decided to endorse her out of Soweto – just like that.' She snapped her fingers.

'But where to? Where did she go?'

'She was sent to the Transkei because her father is a Xhosa.'

'They separated her from her family?' Candy asked, horrified.

Becky nodded without replying. Candy saw that her lower lip was trembling slightly and she remembered that the girl had been Becky's best friend.

'They can't do that to people,' she exploded, feeling all the angrier for not knowing how to comfort Becky.

Raising her face, Becky managed a small smile at the naivety of the statement. 'Too many people get endorsed out of Soweto all the time,' she said.

'What's happened to your friend now? Have you heard from her at all?'

'Her mother got some news the other day. She's in a re-settlement village, but there's hardly any water or food, and there's no work. I don't know what she's going to do.'

'Listen . . . if I gave you some money for her, would you be able to send it, do you think?'

Becky hesitated, as if she was suddenly afraid that she had been thought to have been begging on her friend's behalf. However, Candy had already opened her wardrobe and extracted the fifteen rand she had withdrawn from her post office savings account. She had intended to buy Becky a book token with it so she could get some of the textbooks she still needed. But that could wait; obviously the friend's needs were more urgent.

'I'm sorry it's not much,' Candy said. 'Still, I guess it's better than nothing.' As Becky continued to look doubtful about taking the money, she added, 'We've got to help her.'

'Yes. But it's a lot of money. Are you sure you . . .?'

'Of course.' Candy didn't want to discuss it further, aware that under the circumstances, fifteen rand was really hopelessly little. And then a new, disturbing thought struck her.

'What about you?' she asked. 'Will you be able to get a pass all right?'

'I should be okay. I qualify under Section Ten so . . . But you never know . . . Anyway, I'll see my friend gets this.' Becky held up the money. 'Thank you very much.'

Candy mumbled something and fished under the bed for the large chocolate egg she had bought Becky. The following Sunday was Easter and they had agreed not to see each other then because transport was a problem on public holidays. And also, as Becky had said, 'There might be lots of drunk *tsotsis* hanging about the streets in Soweto.'

'Happy Easter.'

Becky stared in surprise at the egg which had suddenly appeared on her lap, but made no move to touch it.

'I had to get one with chocolates inside it so there would be enough for your cousins as well,' Candy told her, trying to justify the extravagance of her gift.

'It's so big.'

'Well, you can afford to put on weight, not like me.'

'I haven't got you one,' Becky said, shaking her head.

'Thank goodness. I'm not supposed to eat chocolate. It gives me headaches.' Candy watched anxiously as Becky fingered the crinkly cellophane wrapping festooned with showy pink bows and a colourful tag explaining that the egg was home-made from the purest chocolate.

'I can just see my small cousins' faces,' Becky said finally, and she began to mimic them, dropping her mouth open, widening her eyes, and clapping her hands excitedly.

Candy laughed, partly in relief. For a moment she had thought Becky was going to say she couldn't accept the egg.

'You know,' Becky went on, 'they're little monkeys, for sure, those two. Remember the eggs I bought them for Easter a long time ago? Well, I thought I had hidden them extra carefully, but they found them.'

'Serves you right,' Candy teased. 'You shouldn't have bought the eggs so early.'

'Maybe. But I had money then. I didn't know if I would have enough later.'

'Oh.' Candy sat down on the bed.

They were both silent for a few moments, then Becky said, 'Hey, I must think of something to give you for your birthday. What would you like?'

'Perhaps you could give me a pass,' Candy suggested.

Becky burst out laughing. But almost immediately she became serious again. 'I'll have to make you something extra special,' she decided thoughtfully.

* * *

Candy spent Easter Sunday afternoon playing tennis with her cousin, Lillian, at her home in Houghton which was within cycling distance of Candy's own house.

Candy hadn't seen her cousin for quite some time and she found her little changed. She seemed, if anything, even more spoilt and sillier than before. As soon as Candy arrived, she realized that Lillian had invited her over so that she could show off her latest boyfriend; a lithe, blond, medical student called Derek. He was very good-looking and he knew it. However, as the afternoon wore on, Candy was glad of his company because at least he proved more interesting to talk to than her cousin.

They played a few sets of American Singles, and then the maid brought them some tea and they sat in the shade chatting. Candy kept thinking about Becky and wondering how she was spending the afternoon. It was the first Sunday she hadn't seen Becky since they had met, and Candy hadn't realized she would miss her so much. She found herself wanting to talk about her; but not to Lillian. Lillian would not be interested. Any subject that was even remotely connected with politics was taboo as far as she was concerned. She would think Candy perverse to want to make friends with a black person in the first place. In her book, 'normal', clean-living, decent white people didn't nourish such notions. Candy was almost tempted to mention Becky for that reason, but she dismissed the impulse as being immature as well as pointless, knowing Lillian as she did.

She made some excuse to leave early, having already turned down Lillian's invitation to stay on for dinner and be driven home later by 'Daddy's chauffeur'. She wasn't surprised when Lillian insisted on accompanying her down the long, tree-lined drive to the front gate. She knew her cousin was itching to ask her what she thought of Derek.

'He seems nice enough,' Candy told her with an amused smile. 'He's a decided improvement on Peter, anyway.'

Peter had been Lillian's previous boyfriend – a divorced actor, ten years older than Lillian, whose brief entrance into her life had been both dramatic and traumatic. Lillian's father had finally managed to send him packing under threat of a court order, and it was weeks before Lillian forgave her parents sufficiently to start talking to them again.

'You're just as bad as Mummy and Daddy,' Lillian

whined. 'Peter was the first real man I've been out with. Just because he was divorced and so much. . . .'

'Oh come on, now! That's got nothing to do with it as far as I'm concerned. He wasn't a man at all. He was nothing but a rat, and you know it as well as I do. That's why you fell for him, you might as well admit it.'

Lillian fluttered her eyelashes, as if shocked, and then immediately spoilt the effect by smiling knowingly.

'He was fun,' she said. 'At least he knew how to enjoy himself. And I like my men experienced, if you know what I mean.'

'You're just an incorrigible nympho,' Candy told her, getting on her bicycle.

Taking it as a compliment, Lillian laughed. 'Tell you what. Why don't you come again next Sunday. We haven't seen each other for such ages and ages, and we really ought to keep more in touch. I'm sure Derek could ask one of his nice medical student friends to make up a foursome – it could be a lot of fun, don't you think?'

Candy hesitated, tempted by the offer. Then she shook her head. 'I'm sorry,' she said. 'But I've got someone coming to visit me.'

'Too bad. What about the following Sunday then?'

'No good, I'm afraid. Actually this friend comes every Sunday. Today was an exception.'

'Oh . . .' Lillian's eyes widened. 'A boyfriend, is it?' she asked in a disbelieving tone.

'No, a girlfriend.'

'Oh, well . . . in that case, bring her along.' With an indulgent smile, she added, 'I'm sure Derek knows two nice fellow students.'

The moment of truth had arrived. Smiling back at her cousin, Candy said, 'This friend of mine is an African.'

For the first time that afternoon, Lillian was lost for words. 'You mean . . . she's . . .?'

'That's right,' Candy said curtly.

Lillian stared at her. Finally, she gave a small shrug as if to say it was really none of her business. 'Why don't you put her off and come along anyway,' she said, her smile suggesting that she was prepared to indulge her cousin's eccentricities so long as they didn't interfere with her pleasure.

'I wouldn't want to do that. I like her too much. And as it is, I can only see her on Sundays.'

'But your parents . . . surely they must mind her . . . you know . . .?'

Blushing, Candy said hurriedly, 'Why should they?'

'Well. . . .' Lillian giggled. 'Mummy and Daddy would have a fit. I can just see Daddy's . . .' She broke off, and her blue eyes sharpened suddenly. 'Tell you what,' she said casually. 'I don't mind if you bring her with you. Ask her by all means, if you like.'

Candy understood her cousin's expression only too well; she obviously thought she had found a way of getting back at her parents over the Peter business.

'You're despicable, you know that,' Candy said coldly, and she put her foot down on the pedal and set off up the road without saying goodbye. She heard Lillian call out something behind her, but she pedalled on angrily without looking back.

*　　*　　*

Later that same evening, Candy was trying to make herself do some maths homework when her mother came rushing into her room. 'Guess what, dear,' she said. 'It wasn't drugs, after all.'

Candy looked up irritably. 'I haven't the faintest clue what you're talking about, Mum.' She had been thinking about Becky and Lillian, and had started to feel angry all over again.

'I'm sorry, am I disturbing you? . . . It's just that it's rather sweet really, and I was dying to tell someone.'

Candy was forced to smile at her mother's flushed, excited face. 'I do love her,' she thought, and her anger was immediately replaced by a feeling of guilt.

'No, you're not disturbing me, Mum,' she said. 'Go on, I'm all ears.'

'Well, you know how funny Colin was at lunch, sort of subdued and unusually silent? He looked decidedly odd, you know . . . not like his usual self at all. That's why I thought of drugs.'

'Oh Mum, really.'

Her mother gave a little giggle. 'Maybe it was silly of me. But you do hear such terrible stories of people's drinks being laced without them knowing about it. And it was a public dance he went to last night, not just a private party. There could have been all sorts of funny types there. . . . It's all very well to laugh, but you know, anything is possible these days. There was this article just . . .'

'Okay, okay, I believe you. But what's so exciting then?'

'It's a girl,' her mother said triumphantly, as if she was announcing the news of an important birth.

It took a moment for Candy to catch up on her mother's meaning, and then she experienced a sharp stab of jealousy. Suddenly, everybody around her seemed to be either already attached romantically or falling in love. What was wrong; why hadn't it happened to her? Lillian had had her first boyfriend at the age of twelve, and here *she* was, nearly sixteen and still without a single date to her credit. Of course she wasn't nearly as attractive as Lillian. But surely she wasn't completely unappealing either?

'Is that all,' Candy said sourly, and saw the sparkle in her mother's eyes fade. Immediately contrite, she went on more kindly, 'Colin has gone out with girls before, you know, Mum.'

'Yes. I suppose I'm just an old silly, really.'

The way her mother was looking at her made Candy despise herself even more.

'You're not an old silly at all,' she said. 'Just a funny old romantic,' and she took her mother's hand and grinned up at her. 'Now tell me about her. What's so special about this one?'

Her mother laughed. 'You'll have to ask Colin that. He seems to have fallen head over heels for her. He's bringing her home to dinner on Wednesday – he's never done that before.'

'Who is she?'

'Elaine . . . Elaine . . . What did he say her surname was again? Whitehall, Whitehead – something like that. Do you know her?'

Candy shook her head. 'I don't think so. Did he meet her last night?'

'Yes. I oughtn't to tell you this really because he wanted me to keep it to myself. But apparently she was a blind date. I didn't know he was taking a girl to the dance. Silly sausage that he is, he told me he was going on his own, with a group of his mates – as he calls them.'

'Why? Why doesn't he want anyone to know she was a blind date, for goodness sake?'

Her mother shrugged. 'I don't know, dear. But you know what men are like. They can be funny about things like that . . . Anyway, I suppose I'd better start thinking about what to give her on Wednesday when she comes. Colin will be cross if we don't make a special effort. Perhaps we'd better have steak – that's a safe enough bet, don't you think? So long as I can persuade Tom not to overcook it as he usually does.'

'I think I'll go out for the evening on Wednesday,' Candy said.

'But why, dear?' her mother asked, taking her seriously. 'You ought to stay and meet her. She might be very nice.'

'How could she be?'

'That's not kind, dear. Colin is your brother after all.'

94

'I blame you and Dad for that.'

They both laughed.

'Gosh, look at the time,' her mother cried. 'Dad will be home any minute from golf and I've still got to bath and change. I wish we hadn't agreed to play bridge with Lorna and Steve this evening. I don't really feel like going out. But there you are.' She smoothed back her hair with a quick, nervous movement. 'Now, will you see you get yourself some supper, dear? There's cold beef in the fridge and some left-over salad. Colin won't be here either, I'm afraid. He's gone to visit Elaine.'

She frowned as she leaned forward to look more closely at her daughter.

'Are you sure you'll be all right on your own, dear? You wouldn't like to invite a friend round to spend the evening with you? Dad could run her home when we get back. We shouldn't be late.'

'No thanks, Mum.' The only person Candy felt like seeing was Becky, and that was impossible. 'I'd rather be on my own,' she added, and smiled reassuringly.

'Well . . . if you're sure . . .'

'Yes, I'm sure.'

But when her mother had gone, Candy saw the evening stretching before her, desolate and empty, and she felt more alone than ever before.

*   *   *

Much to Candy's surprise, she found herself immediately warming to Elaine when they met. She wasn't a bit brash, as Candy had suspected she might be. On the contrary, her manner was unassuming and friendly. She wasn't glamorous either, which also surprised Candy. However, she was attractive, Candy decided, especially when she smiled and two deep dimples appeared in her cheeks, and her light grey eyes lit up with a liveliness that wasn't immediately apparent at other times.

Elaine was a hit with the whole family. Candy's mother quickly adored her, and Candy's father was soon won round when Elaine expressed an intelligent interest in his garden. She made him take her on a conducted tour of all his plants, and afterwards Candy saw him glowing as Elaine explained that she thought people who loved gardening were always rather special.

'Oh, I wouldn't say that,' he mumbled, and he got all embarrassed, much to Candy's and her mother's amusement.

But what amused Candy most of all was to see the change that had come over Colin. His normal cockiness seemed to have lost its cutting edge. Falling in love appeared to soften him somehow, and make him more vulnerable to others as well as to himself. He even became sensitive about his pimples and embarked on a sugar-free diet in the hope that it would clear them up. Candy laughed at him, but she began to feel a lot more affectionate towards him now that she realized he had never been as certain of himself as he liked to make out.

The first time Elaine came to dinner, she took the trouble to seek Tom out afterwards in the kitchen and compliment him on his cooking. Candy happened to be there, and she was impressed by the gesture. It was unusual for guests even to notice the black man serving at the table, let alone go out of their way to talk to him.

Tom chuckled and told Elaine she must come again very soon, which made Candy smile, remembering how cross he had been beforehand because her mother had kept worrying at him not to spoil the dinner.

The following morning he told Candy, 'That friendgirl for Colin, she's very nice.'

'Because she likes your cooking?' Candy teased.

He shook his head. 'What you think, Candy? You think I'm stupid?'

'All right then. What makes you so sure she's nice?'

'I'm sure because she's got a very nice face and a curranteed smile. Don't you say so, Miss Cand?'

'Yes, I say so,' Candy admitted. Tom's judgements of people might be simple, but she had usually found them to be accurate.

After Elaine's second visit, Tom said, 'Well, now, Miss Cand. Now a very nice friendgirl has come for Colin, what about you?'

'What about me?' Candy asked, beginning to feel uncomfortable.

'When you going to bring a nice friendboy to the house so I can make a plenty-too-much-special supper for him?'

Candy shrugged. 'What do I want with a friendboy? Boys! Too much trouble, boys,' she said. Then she realized she was quoting Becky, and she had a sudden image of Becky standing in the background, grinning at them both, her brown eyes brightly observant.

As Tom started to laugh, Candy turned away and lifted the lid off a saucepan on the stove. 'I think something's burning,' she said to divert his attention. 'Can't you smell it?'

When Tom didn't answer she looked round and found him studying her thoughtfully. In the gruffly gentle way he had sometimes, he said, 'Never you mind, Miss Cand. Soon a nice friendboy will come. For your party maybe.'

'Maybe I won't have a party,' Candy told him brusquely, and she left the room before he could say anything more. She didn't want to talk about the party which her parents had promised her a long time back for her sixteenth birthday. She didn't want to think about it either.

She went into her bedroom. But there she kept bumping into images of Becky, so she wandered out into the garden and after walking about aimlessly for a while, sat down at the edge of the fishpond.

She looked at the little plaster gnome smiling stonily at her across the water lilies. Becky had said he reminded her of the

97

Minister of Defence, or was it the Minister of something else? Candy couldn't remember. She didn't know the one from the other anyway.

If only she could invite Becky to her party. But how could she? Her parents would never agree to it. Her mother would be far too afraid of someone complaining to the police. And what of all the other guests? – They wouldn't be expecting an African to be there. What if some of them objected and made a scene? And Becky? How would she feel, being subjected to countless curious, even if not openly hostile, stares? . . . No, it just wasn't possible.

But in that case, she really ought not to have a party at all. On principle. And if she didn't? If she cancelled the party, what then? What would her principles demand of her next?

Her principles! When it really came down to it, what were her principles? She wanted Becky to have the same equality as herself. But she could no longer fool herself into believing that Becky could ever be truly equal until she had the vote. And when the overwhelming majority of black South Africans had the vote, the inevitable result would be a black government. And then what would happen to herself and her family, and the rest of the white minority? She could imagine herself changing places with Becky and suffering a form of apartheid in reverse.

But if she wasn't able to accept the idea of a black government, then it was hypocritical of her to talk of wanting Becky to be treated as her equal. In an ultimate sense, her principles were meaningless – a sham. So where did that leave her?

God! Why did it all have to be so damned difficult? She didn't want to think about it any more. She was sick and tired of thinking about it.

She rolled over on to her stomach and stared down into the water. Her reflection stared back at her accusingly. A frightened fish darted away suddenly into the depths, and a ripple ran across her reflection, distorting the features and making her nose look momentarily grotesque.

Never you mind, Miss Cand. Soon a nice friendboy will come.

Was she really unattractive?

'Dammit!' she decided. 'I want to have the party. I need to meet more people, and anyway, it's too late to cancel it now.'

A lot of people had already accepted their invitations, including Keith. Keith was a friend of Colin's who had been to their house a few times. He hadn't paid much attention to her, but perhaps at the party . . .? He had such gorgeous green eyes, and he seemed very sensitive and intense. Just her sort of person. He had said he was looking forward to the party – and what's more, he was coming on his own!

Candy got to her feet and brushed down her school uniform in a decisive manner. If Becky didn't know about the party, what harm could there be?

But that wasn't the point!

And feeling trapped again, Candy guiltily found herself wishing fervently that she and Becky had never met.

*   *   *

The burnished browns and soft amber glows of autumn faded all too fast into the khaki-coloured conformity of early winter. When the weather first turned colder, Becky arrived for her Sunday afternoon visit dressed as usual only in a short-sleeved blouse and cotton skirt, and her old scuffed and torn lace-up shoes. Seeing the goose pimples on her arms, Candy scolded her for not wearing a jersey.

'My mother had washed it and it wasn't dry,' Becky explained.

'But don't you have another one you could wear?'

'I've got a coat. But I didn't think it was cold enough for it. *Moenie** worry, man,' Becky added, grinning. 'I'm okay. I'm tough, you know.'

* *don't*

Candy picked out her warmest jersey and made Becky put it on. 'Keep it,' she told her. 'I can't wear it, it doesn't fit me properly.'

The following Sunday Candy handed Becky two new jerseys which she had bought with her post office savings. 'I came across them when I was tidying out my wardrobe,' she lied. 'I've never worn them because the one is too small for me, and the other . . . Well, I can't wear red, it makes me look anaemic.'

She was afraid that Becky wasn't going to believe her after having been asked the previous week to name her favourite colours. But Becky merely shook her head and said, 'You've given me too much already.'

'Oh, come on. Of course I haven't . . . I don't know if the jerseys are any good to you,' Candy continued hurriedly. 'But I thought you might, perhaps, be able to think of someone who can use them if you can't. It seems a waste for them to go on sitting in my cupboard when they're as good as new and I'll never wear them.'

'Yes,' Becky said, and she put on a bright smile. 'They're super jerseys. Thank you very much. They'll make me look very smart. My family won't recognize me.'

Candy wondered whether Becky's family minded her making friends with a white girl. She would have liked to have asked Becky, but she couldn't quite bring herself to, so she started talking about something else instead.

One particularly cold, windy and wet Sunday, Becky walked into Candy's bedroom and immediately stood still, sniffing the air appreciatively.

'What's the matter?' Candy asked.

Becky grinned. 'No smoke. It smells so fresh in here, but it's also nice and warm. It's quite warm at home too,' she hastened to assure Candy who had started to look worried. 'But it gets very smoky and stuffy when we're all there and the stove is on and we have to board up the windows because of the draughts. This is much better,' and she went and sat down in front of the asbestos panel heater to dry off.

Candy said nothing. To her the room seemed claustrophobic. Against the dull greyness outside, the burglar-proofing bars across the window showed up more starkly, further adding to her feeling of being imprisoned.

If only we could go out sometimes, she thought angrily. *Instead of always having to stay shut up in here Sunday after Sunday.*

There were so many things she would love to do with Becky: play tennis, go and see a film or a play, have tea together in Hillbrow, among other young people and away from her own house and family for once. But there wasn't anything they could do together; anywhere they could go. Even walking to the bus stop – when they weren't breaking any apartheid regulations – invited innumerable stares. And they couldn't even go and sit in the garden when the weather was warm enough for fear of throwing her mother into a panic about the neighbours seeing them.

Candy kept telling herself that none of these things were important. All that mattered was her feeling for Becky, and she was in no doubt about that. Nevertheless, as she found herself wanting to see more of Becky and to share more with her, it became increasingly frustrating that she couldn't. It bothered her too that she could never visit Becky and see her house and meet all the members of her family whom she had heard so much about.

It had begun to seem to Candy as though her friendship with Becky was forcing a form of apartheid into her personal life, and that her feelings were being torn down the middle as a result. She was continually having to choose between Becky and her own social inclinations and interests because Becky's blackness barred her from sharing any of them. Firstly, there was the matter of the birthday party. It was close upon her now, and still Candy couldn't make up her mind one way or the other about it. And she kept having to turn down tempting invitations from her friends because she couldn't take Becky with her. But afterwards, despite herself, she felt both regretful and resentful, imagining herself becoming more and more isolated from the social life around her.

The latest invitation had left her feeling particularly upset and depressed. It had involved an all-day outing with a party of young people, and of course, as fate would have it, it had been arranged for a Sunday.

'You must come,' her friend had urged. 'Mick will be there, and I'm dying for you to meet him. He's awfully nice. He's one of Steve's closest friends. I'm sure you'll like him.'

'You matchmaker,' Candy had said, smiling. Then to give herself time to think, she had asked, 'What happens if the weather is bad? Isn't it a bit risky arranging a picnic at this time of the year?'

'Why? If it's cold or rainy, we can all snuggle up nice and cosy in our lounge at home and *braai** our meat in the fire-place. It will be just as much fun I reckon, if not more so. Could you bring some *boereworst†* just in case there isn't enough? It looks like there will be a lot of people. Steve's going mad and asking everyone he can think of.'

'I'm afraid I can't make it,' Candy had finally decided. 'I've got a friend coming in the afternoon and I can't let her down.'

'Well, tell her to come earlier and bring her. There are going to be far too many boys as it is. Who is she? Anyone I know?'

'I shouldn't think so. Her name's Becky Mpala. She's . . . well, she's an African.'

'Pardon?'

'You know, she's black.' And then Candy had taken a deep breath. 'Actually . . . it would be nice to bring her along if you don't think anyone will object and make her feel uncomfortable.'

* *grill*   † *sausages*

'I . . . uh . . .'

Watching her friend's expression change from astonishment to acute embarrassment, Candy had felt all the angrier for foolishly having allowed herself a brief moment of hope.

'Forget it.'

'No, honestly . . . I mean, I don't mind at all. But I just don't know . . .'

'Forget it.'

'I'm sorry, Cand, really I am. If it was just me . . . But I don't even know everyone who will be coming. And you did ask me if . . .'

'I know,' Candy had sighed. 'Thanks for inviting me, anyway.'

'Perhaps another time?'

'Yes. Sure.' And they had walked back across the school playing fields to their English class in awkward silence.

On the Sunday of the picnic, Candy felt prompted to ask Becky if she thought it would ever be possible for blacks and whites to mix together in a friendly fashion.

'For sure, who can say?' Becky replied offhandedly. 'But I manage to put up with you, so I suppose there's always hope.'

Candy laughed because Becky's teasing expression demanded it of her.

But the problem was, as she told herself afterwards, she wasn't at all sure that she and Becky were managing to have the sort of friendship she had initially hoped they might. And she wasn't even thinking of all the frustrating physical and social limitations surrounding their relationship. She kept remembering her thoughts on the bus going home after her second meeting with Becky in town. She had wondered then how on earth they would be able to continue relating as equals when everything between them was so unequal.

Well, now she was increasingly coming to believe that they couldn't. Becky made her feel so guilty, that was the trouble.

Every time she thought of the conditions under which Becky was forced to exist, she felt unbearably ashamed of being white and wanted to give Becky everything she had. But how could she? She kept giving Becky things that she knew she needed, but she felt that whatever she could give her it was never enough. All she was doing was handing over the odd crumb or two which in no way could compensate for having Becky's slice of the country's cake as well as her own.

But what else could she do? Her conscience compelled her to try and help Becky in whatever small way she could, even though – and this was the rub – she knew that by continually giving to Becky she was taking away from that sense of equality upon which their friendship had been founded. She tried to avoid making Becky feel indebted to her, but a certain constraint was creeping into their relationship all the same.

Candy could see it happening and believed she was to blame. But she couldn't find a way out of her circular conflict. And in her most confused and desperate moments she began to tell herself that the only solution was to stop seeing Becky altogether.

* * *

'A present? For me?' In her sudden fluster, Candy's mother almost spilt the milk as she put the tea tray down on Candy's bedside table.

'It's nothing very much,' Becky told her. 'Just something I made myself,' and a little shyly, she held out the oblong package in her hands.

'But whatever for? . . . I mean . . .'

'It's nothing very much,' Becky assured her again. 'It's just to say thank you for all the lovely cakes and the tea and . . . you know, the biscuits and everything, every week.'

Candy's mother gave an embarrassed giggle. 'Well . . . I . . . it's really very sweet of you. But there wasn't any need to . . .'

By then she had undone the brown paper wrapping and was holding up a wickerwork place mat. 'But it's . . . it's absolutely lovely,' she said. 'Did you really make it yourself? . . . Look dear,' she went on, turning to Candy. 'See the intricate pattern in it. Isn't it amazing?'

'It's beautiful,' Candy agreed, smiling. She could see her mother was genuinely touched by the obvious amount of time and patience that had gone into the making of the gift.

'I do think you're clever,' her mother said to Becky. 'I've always wished I could do something like this.'

'It's not so hard,' Becky said modestly. 'I could show you if you like.'

'Oh no, I wouldn't know where to begin. I'm sure I'd be all fingers and thumbs.'

Becky grinned. 'It's quite easy – it's the truth. What you do is . . .' She took the mat and explained how she had started weaving the strands.

Watching the two of them standing close together discussing Becky's handicraft, Candy couldn't help feeling amused as well as pleased. It was the first time her mother was relating to Becky in such a direct and personal manner.

As Candy got up to pour the tea, she said impulsively, 'I'll go and get another cup for you, Mum.'

'Oh no, dear, don't bother,' her mother said immediately. 'I've already made tea for Dad and me. I'd better go and see to it now, before it gets cold.'

'Let him pour his own for once and stay and have tea with us.'

'No, I can't, really dear. I have things to do.' Looking flustered again, Candy's mother smiled briefly at Becky. 'Thank you so much for this mat. It's really lovely,' she told her, and she went away without waiting for Becky to reply.

'Well, all the more cake for the two of us,' Candy joked feebly, trying to shrug off her disappointment. After a moment, she added seriously, 'You are a dark one, aren't you?'

Becky laughed loudly. 'You mean you've only just noticed?'

'No . . . you clot. I mean I had no idea you had such creative talent.'

'I told you I was a Zulu,' Becky said.

Candy glanced at her anxiously. Becky's cheerful, even slightly overwrought manner this afternoon seemed unnatural somehow, as though she was forcing herself to be entertaining and humorous at all costs. She kept laughing very loudly and saying things which were meant to be funny, but the way she said them – with an almost desperate edge to her voice, disturbed Candy and left her uncertain how to react.

Guiltily, Candy wondered whether Becky had found out about her birthday party on the following Saturday and was feeling hurt at not having been invited. But that was silly; there was no way that Becky could have heard about the party. 'I'm just being edgy and imagining things,' Candy told herself firmly.

As if to confirm her conclusion, Becky looked up just then and gave her a sparkling smile. 'I've got a present for you as well,' she said. 'For your birthday. It is next Sunday, isn't it?'

'Yes . . . But you really shouldn't have got me anything.'

'I didn't. I *made* you something. I only hope you like it, that's all.' Becky dug into her satchel and produced a cylindrical object wrapped in newspaper. 'I brought it today because you'll be busy with your family and people on your birthday, and so it will probably be better not to see you then.'

Candy nodded, blushing. She had been thinking the same thing, but for a different reason. She was afraid that if Becky came the following Sunday she might notice signs of there having been a party the night before.

'Well, Happy birthday,' said Becky. 'Go on, open it. It won't bite.'

Slowly, almost unwillingly, Candy stripped away the newspaper to reveal a wooden pen and pencil holder which she realized at once was hand-carved because its smooth, slightly rounded sides were not quite symmetrical. The outside of the holder was decorated in a tortoise-shell design, lightly burnt into the wood. As Candy turned the object round, admiring it, she found that her name was part of the design on one side.

She looked up at Becky, not knowing what to say.

'I'm afraid it's not very good,' Becky apologized. 'I made a few mistakes here and there.'

Candy couldn't see any flaws in it at all. 'It's . . . it's incredible. How on earth did you manage to shape it so beautifully? It's so smooth, and the design is so . . . It's just altogether fantastic.'

She stretched out and hugged Becky fiercely. 'Thank you,' she whispered. And then, to her astonishment, she felt something warm and wet and ticklish running down the side of her neck. Fearfully, she pulled back to look at Becky and found that she was crying.

It was the absolute silence of Becky's grief, the way she sat there without uttering a single sound as the tears streamed down her face, that was so awful.

'What's the matter? What's wrong?' Candy asked hoarsely.

Becky shook her head helplessly. Struggling free of Candy's grasp, she wiped her face on the sleeve of her jersey. 'Nothing,' she gulped. 'It's nothing really . . . Have you got a tissue?'

Candy found her one, and waited, with a feeling of painful suffocation in her chest, as Becky blew her nose.

'I'm okay now,' Becky said, and she grinned through her tears to prove it.

The wet streak down Candy's neck burned her like a brand. In a small, tight voice, she asked, 'Is it me? Have I upset you?'

'No, it's nothing. I'm okay now . . . I'm glad you like your present. Clay might have been better but I thought wood would be stronger, and also that it would go nicely with your desk.'

'It will. It'll look really good.' Candy picked up the holder to admire it again, but she had to put it down because her hand was trembling. 'Becky . . . please tell me what's the matter . . . what made you cry.'

Becky's face contorted in her effort to stifle a sob. 'I . . .' She swallowed desperately a few times. 'Something happened on the way here, that's all,' she managed finally.

Candy's brief moment of relief was immediately replaced by fresh fears. 'What? What happened? Was it the police?'

Becky opened her mouth to speak, then bit her lip, shaking her head slowly with her eyes tightly closed. Candy placed her hand over Becky's rigidly clenched fist.

'Please tell me,' she pleaded softly, 'so I can help.'

'If you . . .' Becky had to clear her throat before she could go on. 'If you must know, I got . . . I was assaulted.'

'Assaulted? Somebody attacked you, you mean?'

'You know . . . raped,' Becky said with great difficulty, and she turned away and buried her face in her hands.

Candy gaped at her, paralysed with shock. Of all the terrors that haunted her imagination, rape was by far the most frightening. It was only when she saw Becky was crying again that she was able to move. She put her arms round Becky, but she still couldn't speak.

Eventually, Becky gave a shaky laugh and asked, 'Have you got any more tissues?'

Candy gave her the box. Then she stood up and poured Becky a cup of strong tea. 'It isn't true,' she told herself. It couldn't be true. Becky was exaggerating. If she had actually been raped, she would have been marked in some way, perhaps bleeding. But her dress wasn't even torn. It didn't seem possible that she could have survived such a personal act of violence without showing any visible signs of scarring.

Feeling slightly reassured, Candy was able to ask, 'Are you all right? You're not hurt or anything?'

'No,' Becky said, calmer now; and Candy decided thankfully that she must have been exaggerating after all.

Putting down her cup, Becky added, 'They didn't hurt me.'

Candy's heart turned back into ice. 'They? . . . How many?'

'Two. I tried to run but they caught me. So what could I do? If I had struggled they would have hurt me. It was horrible, but at least they didn't hurt me.'

'And they actually . . .?' Candy couldn't bring herself to say the word. Even the mere sound of it felt like an assault.

'I told you,' Becky said abruptly. 'But I'm okay. And it's over now.'

'Did you go to the police?'

'The police? What do you think they'd do? Anyway, if I reported the boys, they *would* hurt me.'

'You know who they are then?'

'They used to go to my school. Now they just hang about the streets making trouble. They've done the same thing to other girls. What do they care? Nobody can stop them.'

'But . . . What about your uncle? Couldn't he do something?'

'What? What could he do?'

'I don't know. Talk to them maybe. Tell them he'll go to the police if they don't leave you alone.'

Becky was horrified. 'You mad? They'd laugh at him; maybe they'd stab him.' She shrugged. 'I wouldn't tell him about it. He'd only get worried.' For a moment, it seemed as if she was going to start crying all over again.

'Becky . . . Oh God, I'm so sorry.' Candy clutched Becky to her in a tight hold of despair. She felt she couldn't take any more; she couldn't cope; it was all too much. 'Are you sure you're okay?' she mumbled. 'You don't need a doctor or anything?'

'I'm all right, I told you,' Becky said with a sharp edge to her voice. 'I'm tough. And anyway, it wasn't the first time.'

'Not the . . . you mean it's happened before?'

'When I was twelve. A man – a *tsotsi* – caught me on my way to visit a friend in the evening. He was terrible. He hurt me, and when I screamed he half-strangled me. But, you see, I survived.' She grinned unhappily, smoothing down her skirt as though she was wiping off a memory.

Candy had stopped listening. She didn't want to hear any more. She couldn't bear to know any more; the weight of knowing was too great. She had a sudden frenzied desire to rush off somewhere, anywhere where she could find some fun and forget.

As if from a distance, she heard herself saying almost calmly, 'You know, I think perhaps we oughtn't to see each other for a few weeks – at least until these boys have stopped hanging about. I mean, now that they've caught you once, they might wait for you every Sunday.'

Becky was silent. Candy knew she was staring at her, but she couldn't bring herself to look up and meet Becky's eyes.

'Maybe,' Becky said finally. 'Anyway, you'll be busy with your birthday next week, and I've got some things to do for the next two or three Sundays. So . . . We'll leave it at that. Okay?'

Candy hesitated. '. . . Okay. I'll write to you after my birthday to arrange a date for the next meeting.' Making up her mind suddenly, she crossed the room to fetch the present she had hidden behind her desk.

'This is my birthday present for you.'

Becky shook her head violently, keeping her hands at her side, as Candy tried to give her the enormous parcel. 'It's your birthday, not mine,' she said.

'I know, but I always give other people presents on my birthday. I always have done. It's the truth. It's a sort of family tradition.'

Unsmiling, Becky accepted the parcel and unwrapped it. 'It's a very smart satchel,' she said. 'Thank you very much.'

'I thought you deserved a new one after all these years,' Candy told her, feeling foolish and angry with herself, and with Becky for not understanding that she had to give her the satchel now as they wouldn't be seeing each other for a while.

'Well . . . I must go,' Becky said.

'Don't you want some more tea first?'

'No. I want to get home. I don't feel . . . you know . . . very clean. I want to have a good wash.'

'Yes, of course,' Candy mumbled, ashamed at not having thought of that herself. 'Stay and have a bath here – I'll get you a towel, I've got some lovely bubble bath stuff you can use.' She was about to dash off, but Becky stopped her.

'I'd rather get home,' Becky insisted.

Candy didn't try to persuade her otherwise. She really wanted Becky gone as much as Becky obviously wanted to leave.

They walked to the bus stop mainly in silence, and luckily they didn't have to wait long before Becky's bus came.

'*Sala kahle* then,' Becky said.

'*Hamba kahle*,' Candy replied as she always did. But this time she felt as if she wasn't merely telling Becky in Zulu to 'go well' and safely home.

As usual, Candy waited to watch the bus out of sight. Only then did she begin to understand what had happened that afternoon, and what she had done. For a few seconds, her anguish was so intense that she almost started running after the bus.

But she checked herself, and blinded by her sudden tears, she turned away from the traffic to walk home desolately through the early dusk.

5

Candy put down the cans of Coke and beer she was carrying, and glanced round the crowded room.

'They all seem to be enjoying themselves, don't they?' Elaine said.

Candy nodded. 'Everybody but me,' she thought glumly.

'It's a lovely party,' Elaine continued. 'I congratulate you. It's not often they get going so quickly.'

'Thanks.' Candy looked for Keith and saw him standing near the window, talking to the same blond girl he had been dancing with earlier. 'Do you know who that girl is over there?' she asked Elaine as carelessly as she could. 'The one in the blue dress, talking to Keith?'

'Oh, her . . . That's Celia.'

'Do you know her?'

'Not really. I only met her last weekend at Keith's house.'

'Are they going out together?'

Elaine smiled. 'It seems so. I don't think they've known each other very long though. Why? Why do you ask?'

'Just curious.' Candy turned her back and unsteadily re-filled her glass. 'It serves me right for building up false hopes,' she told herself angrily. But she couldn't help feeling disappointed and hurt all the same.

Elaine leaned closer. 'Hey, you don't fancy Keith, do you?'

'Of course not,' Candy mumbled.

'He certainly is good-looking, but somehow I wouldn't have thought he was your type.'

Before she could stop herself, Candy asked, 'Why not?' and then blushed as Elaine smiled again, knowingly this time.

'I find him a bit odd,' Elaine said. 'I never know what to

say to him. He seems closed up and sullen, as if he's got a chip on his shoulder.'

'Don't you think he's just shy?'

'Maybe . . . Oh, by the way, your mom said I was to tell you not to forget about the sausage rolls in the oven.'

Candy pulled a face. 'She's told me herself three times already.'

'But she really is trying ever so hard to keep out of the way,' Elaine said, laughing. 'You know, I popped into the dining-room just now to see if they wanted anything, and as I opened the door there was this rustling, and there they both were, sitting still as stones, pretending to be absorbed in their newspapers.'

'Dad's okay. It's my mom who gets in a tizz about these things. She's probably driving my dad mad, worrying that we're all getting drunk or breaking things, or running out of food or whatever. Which reminds me, did Colin get some more records?'

'He's gone to get them now. He'd better be back soon or I'll want to know what he's been up to.'

'Well, come and help me make a selection to be going on with, will you? They seem to be into the fast stuff at the moment.' Standing around doing nothing, Candy was beginning to feel like a wallflower again.

Still, she couldn't really complain, she decided, as she and Elaine threaded their way through the dancers to the other side of the room where Colin had set up his hi-fi equipment. At least her worst fear had not been realized; she had already had a few dances, even if only with Colin and the steady boy-friends of one or two of her classmates.

While they were sorting through the pile of records, Elaine suddenly said, 'I believe you have an African girlfriend.'

Candy's heart turned over uncomfortably. She had been trying not to think about Becky. 'Yes,' she said cautiously. 'Who told you?'

'Colin mentioned it. I'd love to meet her. Perhaps you could both come over for a swim sometime when it's warm enough. You haven't been to my house yet, have you?'

'No.' Candy glanced towards the corner where Lillian was flirting in an ostentatious manner with her newest conquest, a red-haired rugby player. Suspiciously, she asked Elaine, 'Why do you want to meet her?'

'I don't know any Africans of my own age. It would be interesting to meet one and find out what. . . .'

'Meet one what?' Colin demanded, appearing suddenly and grabbing Elaine round the waist.

Elaine tried to wriggle free, giggling. 'A decent, good-looking male with manners, like that gorgeous guy over there. Cand and I were just saying that he looks . . .'

'Which one? I'll go and punch his face in.' However, instead, Colin nuzzled Elaine's cheek. 'You know,' he told her, grinning at Candy, 'I don't know what it is about sixteenth birthdays, but my little sister doesn't look at all bad this evening. Not bad at all, don't you think?'

Elaine nodded. 'But then it's always been obvious to me who inherited all the good looks in your family.' And she ruffled his hair fondly.

He was about to reply when something or someone caught his attention behind Candy. Elaine glanced towards the same spot and started to smile, then both of them backed off hurriedly.

Candy turned round to find herself looking up into the shy grin of a tall young man. It was his height more than any-thing else which made her certain she hadn't seen him before that evening. He must have just arrived. She thought she had heard the doorbell ring, but she hadn't done anything about it because her father had told her he would answer the door to latecomers in case gatecrashers turned up.

'Uh . . . hallo,' she said.

He spoke very softly; it was difficult to make out what he

114

was saying. But she caught her own name and something that sounded like 'birthday', so she smiled and said, 'Thank you.'

He had rather a nice face. However, it was his eyes that drew her attention. They were dark and glowing – gentle, expressive eyes. There was something about their colour and shape that reminded her of . . . of . . . No! Not Becky. She was not going to think about Becky tonight.

'I'm Dick,' she thought he said next.

'Pardon?'

This was getting ridiculous. Someone had turned up the volume of the record-player and now she couldn't hear him at all. She pointed towards the turntable.

He laughed, and pointed, first at her, then at himself, and finally at the people dancing in the middle of the room.

'Oh.' Candy nodded vigorously, grinning, and turned to lead the way.

She took him as far away as possible from the loudspeakers, and they started jerking about to the frantic rhythm of the record.

'I'm afraid I didn't catch your name properly before,' Candy began. 'Did you say it was Dick?'

'No, Dirk.'

'Dirk?'

'*Ja*, Dirk de Villiers.'

Candy's feet faltered, lost the beat. She could hear him plainly enough now, and his accent was unmistakable – the soft rolling of his r's was all too audible.

'You're Afrikaans?'

'*Ja*,' he said.

. . . I hate it. It's the language of oppression; of policemen, government officials; all those people who think because you're black you're a bobbejaan . . .

He was grinning at her selfconsciously, his face reddening, and Candy realized she had stopped dancing altogether.

Hastily, she began to move her feet in time to the music once more.

After a few moments, she glanced at him surreptitiously. What on earth was an Afrikaner doing at her birthday party? Who could have brought him without even bothering to ask her first if it was all right? But . . . She glanced at him again. He had his head down, looking at his feet as he swayed and jerked clumsily back and forth, and the soft coloured lights behind him made his face an interesting composition of shadows. He moved like a puppet whose strings had become hopelessly entangled.

As if aware of her amusement, he raised his eyes and started to smile a little foolishly.

'I'm afraid I'm no good at dancing,' he admitted, and for some reason, this time his accent didn't bother her so much.

'You dance just fine,' she told him.

He shook his head and his hair flopped forward over his forehead, giving him a ruffled appearance. 'He should always wear it like that; it suits him,' Candy caught herself thinking, and immediately felt too shy to look at him any more.

When the last record had ended, they remained standing uncertainly in the centre of the room.

'Well . . . thank you,' Dirk said finally.

'Thank *you*.' Candy waited to see if he would say more, and then turned away.

'Uh . . . would you . . . how about a drink?'

Candy stopped. 'That would be very nice,' she said, surprised at how calm and self-possessed she sounded, when she was really feeling so illogically happy and light-headed all of a sudden.

* * *

'Aren't you going to have this scrambled egg, dear? It's getting cold.'

'No thanks. I'm not very hungry.' Candy picked up the half-eaten piece of toast on her plate, and then dropped it again and put her plate to one side. She pulled her cup of coffee towards her, but instead of drinking it, she began to play with her napkin, tying it in knots, only to undo them nervously.

'Must be too much party,' her mother said, giving her a funny look as she took her plate and scraped its remains into a dish for the birds in the garden.

'Probably.'

Candy's stomach fluttered queasily. She kept trying to remember what Dirk looked like, but she could only remember his eyes, and the expression in them as he had said goodbye to her at the front door. Thinking about that, her stomach fluttered again unpleasantly. She had felt beautiful last night; but this morning, when she had looked in the mirror, her nose had seemed to her longer than ever. What if Dirk didn't like her in broad daylight?

'So what?' she told herself. 'If he doesn't like me as I am, he can lump it. I don't even know if I like him yet.' But she didn't feel very convinced, and the next moment she found herself thinking, 'It really doesn't matter that he's Afrikaans.'

It had started not to matter as soon as he had told her he was a first-year Science student at the University of the Witwatersrand. If he had been a diehard Nationalist supporter, he would hardly have chosen to study at an English language university known for its liberal tradition, especially when there was an Afrikaans university nearby.

Unless he was a police spy? She hadn't considered that possibility until now. But no, she couldn't believe it of him. She wouldn't think about it any more. It would only start her thinking about a lot of other things that she wanted to forget, at least for the time being.

'Where's Colin?' her father asked suddenly. 'Isn't it about time he was up?' He sounded tetchy, probably because his Sunday papers hadn't arrived.

117

'He's up and away already,' Candy's mother said. 'He's gone to church, believe it or not.'

'Good God Almighty!'

'Yes, I know. And he even put on a suit for the occasion. Apparently Elaine's young brother is in a Sunday school play or something. I don't know exactly what it's all about, but he's gone to church, anyway. I couldn't believe it myself when he told me this morning.'

'Huh!' But there was a tell-tale twitch at the corner of Candy's father's lips. Next moment, however, he was scowling again. 'Wait a minute. What about the mess from last night. Colin was supposed to help clear up. And those blasted lights. He's got to do something about them before this evening. You can't see a damn thing with them as they are.'

'It's all right, Dad,' Candy said, deciding that this was as good an opening as any for making her announcement. 'A friend's coming to help me get the lounge straight again. We'll manage it all between us . . . Don't worry, I'm sure he'll be able to do the lights.'

'When's he coming, dear?'

Candy was disappointed; her mother didn't sound in the least bit surprised. Colin must have mentioned Dirk to her – that explained the funny look earlier on. With a casual shrug, Candy said, 'In about half an hour or so.'

'Who is he? Anybody we know?'

'Colin must have told you that as well,' Candy teased, and was gratified to see her mother's face redden.

'Oh, no . . . he didn't say anything to me . . . Well, he just mentioned that you had been dancing a lot with somebody last night, that was all.'

'Did he tell you that Dirk is Afrikaans?'

Obviously he hadn't. Her punch line had its effect. Amused, she saw both her parents stiffen slightly.

'Who are you talking about?' her father demanded.

'This friend . . . the one who's coming to help me clear up

after the party this morning. Actually, I've invited him to lunch as well. I hope that's all right.'

'Of course, dear.' Her mother did her best to look delighted at the prospect.

Struggling to keep a straight face, Candy went on, 'I'm afraid his English is terrible, so it would be nice if you would talk a little Afrikaans to him. You know, just so he doesn't feel too uncomfortable.' She knew perfectly well that neither of her parents could speak a word of Afrikaans.

Her father spluttered into his tea. 'Now look here, my girl. Let's get one thing straight. I don't care if you have an Afrikaans boyfriend – that's your business. But when he comes to our house he'll just jolly well have to put up with speaking our language. Do I make myself clear?'

'Actually, Dirk's father is a minister in the Dutch Reformed Church,' Candy said innocently, to further provoke him.

And then, in one of those unexpected, disquieting flashes of insight, she suddenly realized that she wasn't merely playing with her parents. She was trying to punish them, not for their attitudes towards Afrikaners which she, after all, largely shared, but for their lack of support in her friendship with Becky. Immediately, her amusement turned sour inside her.

However, her mother – who could always be counted on to rise to any bait – had already been hooked. 'His father's a Dutch Reformed minister? Which church? Do you know which church, dear? I do hope he doesn't belong to that dreadful group – what do they call themselves again? . . . You know, the ones who believe that the wearing of mini skirts causes drought in the country. I really don't think I could . . .'

'It's all right, Mum, I was only joking.'

'You were? . . . Thank God for that.' Her mother looked across the table at her husband, who took longer than was necessary over wiping his mouth on his serviette.

'I'm not sure that's an altogether appropriate expression to use in this context, girlie,' he finally commented drily.

Candy's mother giggled. 'I suppose not.' She stood up to ring the bell for Tom, then changed her mind and sat down again. 'Is he really Afrikaans?' she asked Candy.

'Yes.'

'Oh dear . . .Well, Ron, it looks like you and I are going to have to learn to talk the *Taal*** in our old age, after all.'

'That'll be the bloody day.'

Candy's mother gave another giggle. 'But he *can* speak English surely, can't he, dear?'

'Yes.' Candy didn't want to talk about it any more.

'How did he come to be at your party?'

'He's friendly with Allan – Eleanor's boyfriend. They brought him along.'

'I see. Well, tell us something about him. What does he do? Is he still at school?'

'No.'

'No?'

'He's a student – at Wits,' Candy said. 'That's how he knows Allan. Now, if you'll excuse me, I'd better go and make a start on the lounge.'

'Wits?' Her mother sounded greatly relieved. 'He couldn't be a rabid Nat then, could he. Not if he . . .'

'No,' Candy said, scraping back her chair.

But her mother hadn't finished yet. 'What did you say his name was again, dear?'

'Dirk. Dirk de Villiers.'

'That's an Afrikaans name all . . .' Her mother broke off as she saw Candy was already walking away. 'Where are you going?' she asked sharply.

'I told you, to begin tidying up the lounge.'

'All right then. But you'd better warn Tom that there

* *language*

120

will be an extra person at lunch – he likes to know these things early. And tell him he can come and clear the table now.'

Candy was half-way down the passage when her mother called her back.

'Yes?' Candy said reluctantly from the doorway, afraid that she knew what her mother was going to ask her. And she was right.

'What about Becky? Isn't she coming as usual?'

'She couldn't make it today,' Candy said, and she dived back into the passage, feeling the stigma of a Judas burning her cheeks.

'A friend for you? Coming for lunch?' Tom asked, carefully pulling the bag of giblets out of the chicken, and holding it up for Candy to see. 'If you like, I'll cook this for your friend, special, Miss Cand.'

'Take it away, Tom, it's disgusting.'

He shook his head. 'You know what, Miss Cand? You're funny, that's all. If you eat this, it will make you very, very, very too much strong.'

'Don't talk nonsense. Take it away, it makes me feel sick. I think it's terrible that we eat animals. It's barbaric.'

'Everybody eat animals, Miss Cand.'

'Well, we shouldn't.'

Laughing at her, he picked up the dish containing the chicken and carried it across to the sink.

'Who's your friend? Is it the one who's coming every Sunday afternoon?' he asked, without turning round.

Candy stared at his back. What did he know about Becky? Suddenly, she lost all interest in telling him about Dirk. 'No,' she said, and made an abrupt move to go.

'Is it a friendboy?'

Candy paused. 'Yes,' she admitted.

'Ha! From your party.' He wiped his hands on his apron, grinning gleefully over his shoulder. 'What did I tell you,

Miss Cand! Didn't I say a nice friendboy would come for your party?'

'You did, yes.'

'What's his name?'

'Dirk.'

'Duck?'

'No. *Dirk*.'

'That's what I said, Miss Cand. Duck.'

Candy shrugged. 'He's Afrikaans,' she said, to get it over with.

'Afrikaans?' Tom's grin contracted into an expression of disgust. 'Poef! That's no good. A Boer is no good as a friend-boy for this house. No . . . no, no good.'

Candy shrugged again, but she couldn't help being amused at the way Tom looked with his nose wrinkled up and his mouth pushed out so that his nostrils nuzzled his upper lip.

'So what if he's Afrikaans, he's nice,' she said firmly.

'You think so?'

'I do,' Candy said with less conviction.

'Maybe.' Tom chuckled. 'Maybe, Miss Cand. But if he's no good, I won't cook any more anything for him. I tell you straight.'

'Okay,' Candy agreed, smiling, and she began to feel nervous and excited again at the prospect of spending the day in Dirk's company.

6

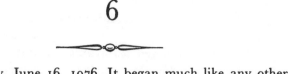

Wednesday, June 16, 1976. It began much like any other
school day for Candy. It was only when she arrived home
from hockey practice in the late afternoon that she heard the
news from her mother.

Violence, involving children, had erupted in Soweto!

'I do hope your friend, Becky is . . .' her mother began,
then stopped as she saw the stricken look on Candy's face.

Candy moved her lips, but no sound came. Becky! She
hadn't seen Becky, nor made any attempt to get in contact
with her for over a month – since the Sunday before the
birthday party when . . . Candy swallowed painfully. 'What's
happened?' she managed to whisper. 'What does the news
say?'

Her mother hesitated. Dimly, Candy was aware of the fear
in her eyes as she finally admitted, 'Well . . . I really don't
know how bad it is, dear. You can't trust the news anyway
– it's so heavily censored. But I think there was a mass
demonstration of schoolchildren and . . .'

'And what?' Candy prompted, barely audible. 'The
police,' she choked on the word, '. . . opened fire?'

'I'm not sure, dear, I'm really not sure exactly what
happened.'

'Was . . . How many dead?'

'I'm not sure, dear,' her mother said again, desperately.
'Listen, why don't you go and get out of your school clothes
while I make us some tea, and we'll see if there are any
details on the radio in a little while.'

Candy stared, her eyes glazed; in her mind she saw
Becky lying in a pool of blood, her body riddled with bullet
holes.

123

'Candy, dear . . .' Her mother stretched out her hand, but Candy shook her off blindly.

'God!' If Becky was dead. If it was too late . . .

'Candy . . .'

'God!' Candy muttered again, and rushed from the room. Flinging herself down on her bed, she covered her face, pressing her fingers into her eyes until her vision went red and the muscles of her eyeballs started to ache.

'Are you all right, dear?'

Her mother's face blurred and shimmered through a mist of whirling, spiralling patterns. Candy blinked violently, as her mother sat down rather gingerly on the edge of the bed.

'I'm sorry, dear. I didn't realize it would be such a shock or I wouldn't have . . . well, you know . . . I . . . I'm sure there's nothing to worry about, though. After all, there are thousands of children in Soweto. The chances of Becky being . . .' Her mother's voice trailed off.

Candy shook her head to clear her vision. She wanted to believe her mother. She wanted to believe that nothing had happened to Becky. Perhaps it wasn't too late after all.

'What was the demonstration about?' she asked weakly.

'It's all to do with this ridiculous Afrikaans business. You know, schoolchildren in Soweto have already been on strike for a month because of it.'

Candy didn't know. She hadn't been following the news at all. She had deliberately closed herself off from anything that might remind her of Becky.

'If only we could get rid of this blasted government,' her mother was saying. 'Before it's too late. Sometimes, I fear it's too late already. I mean, when very young people – mere children – start to . . .' She shook her head in despair. 'You can hardly blame the poor little blighters for going on strike. Why should they be forced to learn in Afrikaans?'

Candy felt her heart sinking into quicksand as her mother

went on to explain about the Department of Bantu Education's proposal to enforce Afrikaans as the teaching medium in half of the subjects currently being taught in English in Soweto schools. There was no doubt in Candy's mind as to how Becky would react to any such proposal. She would be out there demonstrating with the rest of them. And suddenly, Candy was certain that Becky had been killed. Her death was Candy's punishment for having been a coward; for having turned her back on their friendship because it had challenged her complacency and courage and she had lacked the necessary moral fibre to deal with her own inner discomfort.

'Darling . . . Candy, dear, are you all right? . . . Candy? . . .'

Candy stared at her mother, glassy-eyed. 'You're guilty. We're all guilty – can't you see that?' she wanted to shout at her. But she couldn't; she was too terrified of the violence of her own guilt.

Her mother touched her arm nervously. 'Would you like a cup of tea, dear?'

Candy shook her head. She wished her mother would go away. But her mother was obviously afraid to leave her on her own.

After a short silence, her mother said with forced cheerfulness, 'By the way, I forgot to tell you, Dirk rang just before you arrived. He was wondering if you'd like to go to a poetry reading this evening. It could be fun . . . You know, he's such a sweetie, that boy.'

Dirk! Candy shot off the bed. There was something she had to do right away; something she should have done a long time ago.

Her mother followed her to the door. 'Where are you going?' she asked anxiously.

'To ring Dirk.'

'Oh.' Her mother gave a relieved, knowing smile. Only she didn't know, Candy thought.

Fortunately, Dirk answered the telephone himself; she didn't feel in the mood to have to talk to his mother first.

'Can you come over *now*?' she asked.

'*Ja*, of course,' he said, in his soft, gentle voice. 'But why? Is something wrong?'

'Will you leave straightaway?' and she put the phone down.

She waited for him in the garden. As soon as she heard his scooter, she went to the gate to meet him.

'Leave it here,' she told him, and led him across the lawn to the bench, surrounded by shrubbery and out of sight of the house.

'What's the matter?' he asked, but she shook her head, wanting to wait until they were both sitting down before she began.

Dirk seldom smoked, but now he immediately patted all his pockets until he found the packet of Rothmans he always carried around with him. Candy noticed the unsteadiness of his hands when he struck a match and her resolve faltered. He was looking at her, his dark eyes full of anxiety and concern. She fixed her gaze on the glowing end of his cigarette as she struggled to find a way of putting her question less bluntly.

'You know about the trouble in Soweto?' she began.

'*Ja*?'

'You know what it's all about?'

There was a pause before he said cautiously, 'I'm not sure what you mean.'

'I mean . . .' Candy squirmed slightly. 'You know the reason for the demonstration?'

Another pause, and then he breathed out heavily. 'Aahh, I see. This has to do with my being Afrikaans?'

'Well . . . not exactly . . . Well, yes, in a way . . . I . . . it's just that we've never really talked politics and I think it's time we did.'

126

'I see. And if we disagree?' Before Candy could answer, he leaned forward suddenly and stabbed his cigarette out on the grass in a couple of jerky, almost vicious movements. 'We'd better get one thing straight, right away, man,' he said fiercely. 'I'm an Afrikaner, and nobody and nothing is going to make me want to change that.'

His aggressiveness was so out of character that for a few moments Candy was too surprised to feel anything other than a sense of shock.

'I'm sorry,' Dirk went on, no longer angry but not sounding apologetic either. 'That's just the way it is.'

Candy was glaring at him now in open hostility. Without giving her a chance to speak, he explained, 'But because I'm not ashamed of being an Afrikaner, it doesn't mean to say that I support apartheid, or think that the black man – sorry, black people are inferior.'

'No?' Candy said coldly. She couldn't understand or condone his total lack of shame. To her it was like saying you didn't support the official Nazi attitude towards Jewish people, but you were unequivocally proud of being a Nazi just the same.

'Hell, you know,' Dirk was saying, 'being Afrikaans, for me, has not all that much to do with the colour of my skin. The Cape Coloureds are as Afrikaans as I am. They share the same culture, the same language, and their poets speak with the same voice as my favourite white poets. They're Afrikaans to the bone, like me, and I see them as being an integral part of my cultural identity.' He was frowning at the blade of grass he was carefully stripping between his fingers, but his gaze was abstracted, and when he looked up, his eyes were incandescent like . . . like Becky's, Candy thought suddenly. Becky's eyes had burned with a similar passionate intensity that first Sunday in Candy's bedroom when she had talked about Shakespeare, a long, long time ago. Candy caught her breath painfully, but Dirk had already started to speak again.

'You know,' he said, 'I really love my language. Especially its poetry. It gets to me in a way that . . .' He shrugged, unable to put his feelings into words. 'I guess its sentiment is in my blood,' he finished lamely, with an embarrassed smile.

Without stopping to think, Candy shot at him, 'And because you happen to love it so much, you think black schoolchildren should be forced to learn in it, whether they want to or not. Shoot down the bastards if they object; the less of them there are to have to deal with, the better.'

Dirk flinched as if he had been slapped in the face. 'Of course not,' he said in a shocked, angry tone. 'Man, haven't you been listening to anything I've been trying to tell you? I . . .'

'Yes, I have,' Candy said hurriedly. 'I have been listening . . . I'm sorry.'

Dirk shrugged and leaned back. 'I still don't know what all this is about. But if you want to talk politics, okay, let's talk politics. Tell me your views. What are you? A Communist? A Liberal?'

'I don't know what I am, except I know I'm a coward.'

He looked at her, saw that she was in earnest, and that her whole body was rigid and trembling.

'Candy,' he said gently. 'Candy, what's wrong?'

'It's this friend of mine in Soweto,' Candy blurted out. 'Becky. I'm terribly worried about her – that something's happened to her.'

'You think she was in the demonstration this morning?'

'She was,' Candy said with certainty.

He gave her a questioning look, but refrained from asking her how she knew. Instead, he said, 'I can understand you being worried. But out of so many, the chances, you know, of anything having happened to her must be very slight.'

Candy turned her face away. She couldn't explain about her conviction; it would sound silly; and anyway, she couldn't bring herself to talk about it.

'I've got to find out somehow,' she mumbled.

Dirk thought for a moment. 'I just don't know what to suggest,' he admitted. 'Obviously the police won't be any use.'

Candy got to her feet. She couldn't go on sitting still any longer. She had to do something.

'Would you give me a lift to Soweto?' she asked.

Dirk stared at her in horror. 'You can't go there. It's crazy. Anyway, you won't get anywhere near it. There'll be police all over the place.'

'I might be able to sneak in somewhere.'

'You've got to be joking. And if you did get past the police? What then? You wouldn't get two yards before you were stoned to death. You don't stand a chance. The whole township must be in an uproar.'

'I've got to try. If I get as near as I can, there might be somebody who can tell me something.'

Dirk rubbed his hand up and down the back of his hair – a typical gesture when he was feeling uncomfortable or indecisive.

'Okay,' he said, and he uncrossed his long legs and reluctantly followed her across the lawn.

As he was about to start his scooter, he noticed the front tyre was flat. 'Damn!' he muttered. 'I saw it was a bit soft when I left home, but you sounded so upset over the phone I thought I'd better get here as fast as possible.'

Candy gave him a desperate, accusing look. 'Haven't you got a pump?'

He shook his head apologetically. 'Anyway, it must be a slow puncture,' he told her.

Oh, hell! Candy thought. There was her bike, but it would take hours and hours to ride to Soweto, and by then it would be dark. And she didn't know about buses or trains. She would have to get into town first and then try to find out how to get to Soweto from there. That would also take hours.

'Hell!' She punched the padded seat of the scooter hard enough to hurt her hand.

'I'm sorry,' Dirk said. 'If I'd realized it was a puncture, I'd have done something about it. I'm sorry.'

At that moment, Tom appeared in the gateway, returning from one of his brief afternoon visits to a friend in the neighbourhood. Because Tom usually came back from these visits in a very jovial frame of mind, Candy regularly accused him of using his friend as an excuse to slip away for a couple of drinks on the sly in some backyard shebeen.

Now, as soon as Tom saw the two of them, he stopped and began to clown around, staggering sideways and hiccuping loudly, with his head lolling and a glazed, idiotic expression on his face. He was a natural comedian. Dirk burst out laughing, but Candy was too preoccupied with her own thoughts to manage more than a half-hearted smile.

'Hey, Tom,' Dirk called. 'Do you know how to fix a puncture?'

'Me?' Tom pretended to be horrified. 'What you think, Mr Duck?'

'Man, I think I should throw this stupid damn scooter away. It's always going wrong.'

Tom leaned down, his hands on his knees, to inspect the flat tyre. 'Shame,' he said, clucking his tongue sympathetically. 'You better buy a car, Mr Duck, that's all.'

'I would if I had any money.'

'Ha!' Tom straightened up, shaking his head. 'That's no good. A friendboy with no money is no good in this house. Don't you say so, Miss Cand?'

Candy looked at him blankly. 'Sorry Tom, what did you say?'

'He said I must go because I'm too poor to pay a big enough *lobolo** for you,' Dirk told her, grinning.

'Oh.'

* *bride price*

Tom chuckled.

With an effort, Candy roused herself. 'But he does have a nice face, Tom. Don't you say so?'

Dirk put his arm round her and gave her a squeeze, and briefly Candy was able to recognize a feeling of relief in knowing she had been worrying unnecessarily about Dirk's political inclinations all this time.

Tom beamed with delighted approval at them both. 'I say so, Miss Cand. I say he's got a very, very, very curranteed nice face,' and he walked on up the drive, laughing to himself.

'So? What do we do now?' Dirk asked.

Candy pulled away from him, her fear closing in around her again like an invisible fog.

'What about Tom?' Dirk said suddenly. 'Perhaps he could help. He shouldn't have too much trouble getting into the township and if you gave him your friend's address . . .' He broke off as he saw the immediate alarm and consternation on Candy's face.

'How could I ask him, Dirk? What if he was killed? I'd never forgive myself. It can't be very safe for anyone to wander round there at the moment – you said yourself that . . .'

'*Ja*, I know, you can't ask him. It was stupid of me. I wasn't thinking. I'm sorry.'

Candy gave him a glimmer of a smile. He was only trying to be helpful, and she did feel grateful for his concern. After all, he didn't even know Becky. And then, as she looked into his eyes, it suddenly struck her forcibly how much she had actually missed Becky in the past weeks. She had tried to blot Becky right out of her mind, but thoughts about her had kept coming up all the same. And there hadn't only been feelings of guilt involved. She had missed Becky's sense of humour, her vitality and warmth, her uninhibited, giggly, schoolgirlish manner hiding such inner strength and a surprisingly adult sensibility in some respects. She . . .

Dirk had put his hand on her shoulder and was smiling at her anxiously, and Candy realized she must have been staring at him.

'Are you okay?'

Candy nodded. 'I've never told you, but your eyes are so like Becky's. They're the same colour, the same shape, they even have the same expression sometimes.'

'Really?' Dirk laughed. 'Maybe we share the same ancestor somewhere along the line.' He didn't sound at all embarrassed in admitting the possibility. Candy put her hand over his on her shoulder.

'You'd better introduce us,' Dirk told her.

'Yes.' Candy tried to persuade herself that she would have a chance to do so.

'Why don't you try writing to her?' Dirk suggested after a moment.

'But that could take days.'

'I know. There's not very much else you can do right now, though, is there?'

'No,' Candy had to admit miserably. 'I suppose there isn't.'

*   *   *

The unrest and rioting in Soweto continued and began to spread to other black townships throughout the Transvaal. Students at the University of the Witwatersrand went on a protest march in support of the African children's strike and Dirk came round to visit Candy afterwards, covered in paint which had been thrown at him by an onlooker. Candy didn't know whether to laugh or cry as she tenderly tried to remove the worst of it from his hair.

However, for the most part, life in the white suburbs surrounding Johannesburg went on much the same as always. The violence was distant; the police were containing it within the black areas; there didn't appear to be any immediate need for panic. Nevertheless, there was an increase in the sale of firearms, and people were beginning to talk with unusual uncertainty about their own future. South Africa's borders were no longer so secure; in the past few years, neighbouring white controlled governments seemed to have been collapsing like cards. The *swart gevaar** was creeping nearer on all sides; and now it was rearing up with new determination from within the country itself. But so long as the police continued to remain in control of the situation with their usual ruthless efficiency, and the violence wasn't allowed to spill out into white areas, well then, things would surely settle back to normal again in a little while. After all, the white establishment was still more than strong enough to survive unscathed this present period of black unrest, as it had survived similar outbursts of black protest in the past – even if the future did seem less certain now than ever before.

Little of this, however, concerned Candy, fully preoccupied as she was by her fears about Becky. Her brief moment of hope each morning before the mail arrived became more and more difficult to generate as days went by without any reply to her letter. After a week of waiting, Candy wrote a second letter, this time adding 'To Whom it May Concern' on the envelope; for by now she was completely convinced that Becky must be dead.

'But it's much too soon, man, to be so sure,' Dirk tried to reason with her. 'It's more than likely she didn't get your letter. Hell, I don't even know if there is a postal delivery service in Soweto; and if there is, anything could be happening to the mail there in the present upheaval.'

Candy leaned back on the sofa, resting her head against Dirk's arm, and closed her eyes. She wished she could believe him. But she couldn't.

'Tell you what,' Dirk went on, 'I'll have a word with Sarah. I don't know why I didn't think of it before.' Sarah

* *black peril*

was his African maid, a cheerful, middle-aged woman who had been working for Dirk's family for many years – in fact, for almost as long as Tom had been working for Candy's family.

'What can she do?'

'She must have a friend living in Soweto.' Dirk smiled. 'She seems to know a helluva lot of people, there's always somebody visiting her. Give me Becky's full name and address and I'll speak to Sarah as soon as I get home. Don't worry, she'll come up with something, you see.'

Without looking at him, Candy said, 'Will you ask Sarah to try and find out if the family need anything – like money, perhaps.'

'What do you mean "the family"? For Pete's sake, it's completely unreasonable to suppose the worst just because you haven't heard from Becky.'

Candy said nothing. 'Come on now,' Dirk ordered, shaking her gently. 'Snap out of it. Let's go into Hillbrow and have a hamburger. We can go to that place where they have folksinging. You know, the one I was telling you about?'

Candy shook her head apologetically. 'I'm sorry, Dirk, but I honestly don't feel hungry.'

'You will. Just wait till you see their hamburgers. Come on!' He yanked her to her feet; and before she had time to protest, he had strapped her into his crash helmet and was propelling her firmly towards the door.

* * *

A few days later, as Candy wheeled her bicycle through the school gates, she caught sight of Dirk sitting on his scooter at the kerbside, doing his best to look invisible as hordes of girls streamed past him. She went up to him, her face reddening in embarrassment to match his own.

'What are you doing here?' she whispered, acutely conscious of the curious stares all around them.

He grinned awkwardly. 'I've got something to tell you. Get on, will you, and let's get out of here.'

'But . . . What about my bike?'

'Leave it. Chain it to the fence or something.'

Suddenly Candy froze. 'I've got something to tell you,' he had said. The blood drained out of her face.

'Dirk . . . is it about Becky?'

'*Ja*. She's okay. But I'll tell you all about it when we . . .'

Candy dropped her bicycle. She leaped forward and grabbed Dirk's arm, completely oblivious now of her surroundings.

'Are you sure?' she cried.

'*Ja*,' Dirk told her happily, and then he blushed more deeply as some sniggering broke out behind them. 'Go and chain your bike,' he hissed urgently.

'It doesn't matter.' Candy swung up on to the seat behind him. 'If it gets pinched, too bad. Let's go.'

Muttering something inaudible, Dirk went to pick up the bicycle and chained it to the fence for her, pretending not to notice the group of first formers standing nearby who were studying him with unconcealed interest and amusement. Then he came back and started the scooter; they tore off down the road at full throttle.

'We'll go and have coffee, okay?' Dirk shouted over his shoulder.

Candy pressed her cheek against his back, exulting in the force of the wind whipping through her clothes and scouring her skin. She felt all the darkness inside her being swept away, leaving her light-headed and tingling. She tightened her arms round Dirk's middle, squeezing with all her strength, until he shouted back laughingly to her to stop, she was killing him.

'I love him,' Candy thought. 'I love everybody.' Perhaps there was a God, after all. Perhaps God simply was love.

When they reached the steak house, Dirk refused to answer any of her questions until they were seated at their usual corner table with earthenware mugs of strong, steaming coffee in front of them.

135

'So, Becky's okay,' he began. 'You can stop worrying. Sarah's friend – Elizabeth, went to Becky's house yesterday. Sarah really moves fast, you know. I told you she'd come up with something, didn't I?'

'You did,' Candy agreed readily, and she gave him a grateful, loving smile. He was such a sweetheart, a dear, beautiful person; and Becky was alive. Nothing else mattered for the moment.

'I wanted to tell you right away, without losing any time,' Dirk said. 'But . . . whew! . . .' He shook his head slowly. 'Next time, I think I'll wait for you at home. Man, I've never been so embarrassed in all my life.'

Candy laughed. 'It's because you're so good-looking,' she told him, realizing suddenly that although embarrassed herself, she had also felt secretly proud to have been able to claim him in front of so many of her schoolfellows.

'But tell me about Becky now,' she continued eagerly, leaning forward with her elbows on the table. 'Did Sarah's friend actually see her and talk to her?'

'*Ja*. Apparently Elizabeth lives almost in the same street. Talk about luck. She even knows the family slightly. She says Becky's uncle has a shop – is that right?'

'Yes. But go on – what about Becky? Did she get my letters? Does she know I've been trying to get in touch with her?'

'I don't know. Elizabeth didn't tell me very much. But Becky's obviously all right and well and that's . . .'

'But did she . . . did Becky say anything about arranging to meet me? You did tell Elizabeth to tell her I was very anxious to see her and talk to her?'

'*Ja*, I did.' Dirk was beginning to look uncomfortable. He put down his coffee mug and wiped his mouth.

'And? . . . What did Becky say?' Candy asked impatiently. However, she had to wait while Dirk struggled to light a cigarette. Finally, he exhaled a thick cloud of smoke that hid his face for a few seconds.

'Man . . . I'm only going by what Elizabeth said to me, see? I don't know if . . .'

'Yes, yes, sure. Just tell me what she said.'

'Well . . .' Dirk blew out more smoke. 'Elizabeth seemed to think Becky didn't want to see you.'

Candy knew she should have expected this, but it didn't lessen the shock, or the sharp stab of pain. It was a little while before she could speak, and then she mumbled, 'Did she say why?'

'I did ask Elizabeth that, several times. But all she could or would tell me was that Becky was okay and you mustn't write to her . . . and she couldn't see you.'

'Couldn't or wouldn't?'

'Elizabeth said *couldn't* to begin with. But after I kept asking her if she knew why Becky couldn't see you, she got all embarrassed and finally admitted that Becky had told her she didn't want to see you. But I wasn't able to get any more out of her than that . . . I'm sorry. Hell, I just don't know . . .' He shrugged. 'Would you like some more coffee?'

Candy shook her head. She was silent for some time, staring down at her hands. Eventually, all she said was, 'I don't blame her.'

'You know, it occurred to me . . . It's always possible, I suppose, that Becky might be in some kind of trouble with the police. Have you thought of that? I mean, maybe she's under surveillance and that's why she says she won't see you and you mustn't write – she doesn't want to get you involved.'

Candy looked up at him, feeling her fear slice through her like an ice scalpel, freezing as it cut. If the police were keeping a watch on Becky, then they would most likely know about the two letters she had written to her. In which case. . . .

Candy tried to remember exactly what she had put in the letters . . . *I'm terribly worried about you . . . Please let me know how you are . . . I must see you . . .*

I must see you – what would the police make of that? Why did she have to see Becky? To pass on or receive important information? To discuss strategy? Candy remembered that she had underlined *must* several times. There had also been other things she had said that could sound equally suspicious if you chose to interpret them in a certain way. Perhaps the police were keeping a watch on her now as well. Perhaps they were . . .

'Was Becky involved in anything?' Dirk asked anxiously.

'What do you mean?'

'Well, did she belong to any organization, or was she doing anything that could be described as subversive?'

'No. Not as far as I know.'

But would Becky have told her if she was? Candy thought immediately. Probably not. After all, she had never given Becky any reason to believe she could trust her with such information.

Dirk looked relieved. 'I wouldn't worry too much then,' he said. 'If you don't know anything, you can't really be implicated, even if the police do have something on Becky. As far as you're concerned, she was giving you Zulu lessons and she came to your house once a week for that purpose. That's all there is to it – should the police question you, which I'm sure they won't.'

That's all there is to it. The words were meant to reassure, but Candy heard them as her own accusing voice echoing back to her through the blinding mist of her fear.

'No!' she almost shouted. 'That's not all there is to it.' And having admitted the fact, she felt instantly calmer and more in control of herself. 'God! We're all so damned afraid, aren't we,' she muttered.

Dirk tried to say something but she went on fiercely, 'I've got to see Becky. If she's in trouble, then maybe there's something I can do to help. I don't know . . . But I've got to talk to her.'

Dirk helped himself to another cigarette. 'It's up to you,' he said. 'But I don't think you should do anything just yet. And anyway, how are you going to manage to see Becky when she obviously doesn't want to see you at the moment?'

'I don't know. I'll think of something. In the meantime, I'll try another letter. I'll be very careful what I put in it, but somehow I have to persuade her to meet me.'

'Can't you wait at least until we get back from the sea? Hopefully, things might have calmed down a bit by then.' Dirk and Candy and her parents were shortly due to leave for the Natal South Coast to spend ten days in a beach cottage which Candy's family rented each year during the winter holidays.

'It's only a few weeks,' Dirk pointed out.

'No! It can't wait that long,' Candy cried. 'You don't understand.'

'I do,' said Dirk, at last beginning to lose his patience. 'Man, I know you feel you let Becky down and you want . . .'

'That's only half of it.'

'*Ja?*'

'I let myself down, don't you see? That's the worst part.'

Dirk looked at her in silence with his eyebrows raised. Finally, he nodded thoughtfully.

'*Ja.*' He sighed. 'It's a helluva life, isn't it.'

Candy found herself smiling a little at the way he said it. After a moment, he also smiled.

'Well, if you're ready, let's go, hey,' he said.

7

Candy propped her bicycle against the wall and, taking off her school hat, wiped her hair back from her eyes.

The open garage doors framed a view of the garden. Candy noticed that the buds, swollen like arthritic knuckles on the branches, were already starting to crack into green. She breathed in deeply: the air smelt dusty, acrid. If spring was just around the corner, she couldn't feel it in herself.

It was ridiculous, she realized, to be so tired when she had only been back from holiday a few weeks. But she couldn't shake off the sense of defeat which hung over her like a heavy thunder cloud, making her headachy and listless, and reluctant to go into the house and face her mother's cheerfully conscientious questions about her day at school.

Dirk's right, Candy told herself. *There's nothing more I can do now. I've just got to accept that I've failed, and I'll never see Becky again.*

She had written several more letters to no avail; and then Dirk had asked Elizabeth to call in at Becky's house again. The situation in Soweto was still far from calm, and there had been further pockets of black unrest all over the country. The continuing disturbances had caused many more deaths and resulted in hundreds, if not thousands, of arrests, and Candy had been plagued by new fears for Becky's safety. But for all that, she hadn't been able to bring herself to the point of actually trying to get into Soweto. Anti-white feeling there would still be running high, and it didn't take Dirk long to convince her that any such action on her part would not only be suicidal, but also completely pointless when Elizabeth lived so close to Becky and wouldn't mind, he was sure, going to check up that she was still all right.

This time, Candy had seen to it that she was there when Elizabeth came back to report on her findings.

'She okay, medem,' Elizabeth had assured her.

'Did you give her my note?'

'Yes, medem.'

'And?'

'Medem?'

'Did she say anything . . . did she tell you if she was in trouble with the police?'

'Aaiiee! . . .' Elizabeth had tugged at her headscarf, giggling in embarrassment and looking everywhere but at Candy's face. 'No, medem, she not frightened for the police. I'm very sorry, medem, she just say it no use to see you, that's all. I'm very sorry.'

'Yes,' Candy had mumbled. 'I understand.' This was the confirmation she had been dreading. Becky despised her and didn't want to have anything more to do with her, now or ever.

The conversation with Elizabeth had taken place not long after Candy's return from the coast. Since then, she had been trying to make up her mind whether to write one last letter to Becky; a letter of explanation, expressing all the thoughts and feelings which had been bottled up inside her for so many weeks. If she was never going to see Becky again, Candy at least wanted her to know how sorry she was for having been such a failure as a friend.

Finally, last night, in a very low frame of mind, Candy had sat down to write the letter. But after reading through the ten pages she had written and rewritten several times over, she found she had failed to express herself adequately; and afraid of being misunderstood, she had torn the letter up and crawled dejectedly into bed, only to toss and turn for what seemed like hours before sleep had finally come. Then she had had a nightmare . . .

She was walking down Eloff Street in Johannesburg. Individuals around her started becoming aggressive, jostling her as she went past. Suddenly, fighting broke out, and people began attacking one another indiscriminately. Terrified, she tried to run away, but wherever she turned, somebody blocked her path, threatening to kill her. In a state of near hysteria, she eventually found a narrow alley-way and plunged into it, sobbing and gasping for breath. However, she had barely gone a few yards down it when she heard her name being shouted behind her. She pulled up and turned round fearfully; and there was Becky, lying on her back on the ground with two white youths standing over her, attacking her with knives.

'Help me,' Becky screamed. 'We're friends, aren't we?'

Desperately, Candy looked round for a weapon, and saw a pistol lying nearby in a pool of blood. Grabbing the pistol, she charged the youths, shouting and swearing at them for all she was worth. Just before she reached them, they backed off laughing, and ran away.

Becky scrambled to her feet, grinning. 'Thanks,' she said. 'By the way, that's my gun,' and she held out her hand.

Candy gave her the pistol, feeling faint with relief that Becky wasn't badly hurt.

'Thank you very much,' Becky said warmly. Then immediately her expression hardened, and she pointed the gun straight at Candy.

'But . . . we're friends,' gasped Candy.

'It's the truth,' Becky agreed. 'But it has to be you or me. There isn't room for both of us.'

As she was about to pull the trigger, Candy shouted, 'No! . . . Please . . . It's not too late . . . Please! . . .'

Becky hesitated. 'I'm very sorry,' she said, and then the gun went off.

Candy's screams had woken her up. For a long time she had lain unmoving in a sticky sheath of sweat, crying compulsively and silently into the pillow . . .

There was a patch of oil on the garage floor; a dull, dark stain like dried blood.

Blood, on her hands, the gun slippery in her grasp . . . 'That's my gun' . . . Becky's expression hardening, then softening again . . .

'I'm very sorry' . . . *A split-second poignancy of shared sadness and regret more intense than even the terror of death* . . .

Candy blinked and tried to swallow. Her throat had closed up. She leaned back against the wall, clutching at her chest until the tightness eased.

It was only a dream – a ridiculous nightmare.

A brief scurrying sounded suddenly from the rafters overhead. A rat perhaps. A rat! . . . Candy leaped away from the wall and peered up nervously, but it was too shadowy to see properly.

'It's probably only a mouse,' she told herself. 'Don't be such a sissie.' Nevertheless, she didn't feel inclined to stay and find out. Lifting her briefcase off the carrier on her bicycle, she hurriedly left the garage; and then walked more slowly round the side of the house to the front door.

Her mother came rushing out of the lounge to meet her in the hall.

'You're back. Thank goodness!' she cried. 'Becky's here. She's waiting for you in your room. She looks terrible.' Her mother paused only long enough to take a quick breath. 'She's hardly said a word since she arrived, and she won't let me make her anything to eat. I do hope nothing's . . .'

But Candy was already tearing down the passage.

Becky stood with her back towards the doorway, staring out of the window. Something about the set of her shoulders made Candy slow down and stop before she reached her.

'Becky?'

Becky turned and looked at her, unsmiling.

'Becky, God, am I glad you've come. I thought I'd never see . . .'

'I haven't come to see you,' Becky said coldly. 'I've come to ask you a favour.'

She did look terrible, but it wasn't just that she had lost weight and was almost painfully thin. Her face had altered in some subtle way that had nothing to do with its overall shape. It seemed to have lost its liveliness and mobility, as if the muscles and flesh had set hard against the bone, giving the face the rigid appearance of marble.

Candy made a move to touch her, but Becky immediately stepped back out of reach, and Candy dropped her arms awkwardly to her sides again. She stopped smiling and said quietly, 'I'm glad – that you've come to ask me a favour, I mean. What is it?'

'I wouldn't have come, only there wasn't anywhere else to go.'

Candy nodded, feeling hurt but determined not to show it. 'Tell me how I can help.'

'I need some money.'

'Sure. How much do you need?' Candy could barely keep her relief out of her voice. She had been afraid Becky was going to say she was on the run from the police and needed sanctuary.

With a shrug, Becky turned away towards the window again. 'Quite a lot. Maybe thirty, forty rand – if that's possible.'

'I've got fifty rand in the post office you can have. But it'll take a day or two to get it. Did you want the money now?'

Another shrug. 'It can't be helped,' Becky muttered. 'A few more days won't matter.'

Candy went to the wardrobe for her purse and emptied it out into her hands

'There's about seven rand here,' she said. 'Will it help in the meantime?'

'Yes, thank you.' However, Becky remained standing where she was, and Candy had to walk right up to her to give her the notes. As their eyes met briefly, Candy saw what it had cost Becky to have to come to her like this.

'I'm sorry, Becky.'

'Why?'

'For everything,' Candy wanted to say, but the hostility in

Becky's eyes and voice stopped her. Lamely, she mumbled, 'I'm sorry if things are rough at the moment.'

Becky's grating laugh unsettled her, but she went on, 'Is there anything else you need?'

'Freedom,' and Becky laughed again without humour.

'Yes.' Candy walked to the bed and sat down, resting her head on her hands. 'When do you want to come and get the money?' she asked after a short silence.

'I can't come tomorrow, or the next day. Better make it the week-end, if that's okay?'

'Of course. I'll see I have it ready for you then.'

They looked at each other across the width of the room. Candy started to smile hesitantly, and a brief flicker of response ran through Becky's face, relaxing her grim expression slightly. For an instant, sharp shadows of pain were clearly visible in her eyes before they narrowed again into the concentrated focus as of someone taking aim down a gun barrel.

'Thank you,' Becky said, and she started towards the doorway. 'I'll pay you back as soon as I can get a job.'

'Wait! . . . It's fine. Don't worry about that. Listen, I . . .'

'I don't want charity,' Becky snapped. 'It's a loan. I'll pay it back. So long as you don't need it straightaway.'

Candy shook her head, desperately trying to think of some way of making Becky stay a little longer.

'Okay then. I'll see you on Sunday,' Becky told her.

'Hang on!' Candy jumped up and placed herself between Becky and the door. 'Do you have to go now? Can't you stay and have some tea? There's so much I want to . . .'

'No, thank you. I'm in a hurry.'

'Well, won't you at least tell me what's been happening to you?'

Becky hesitated. A struggle seemed to be going on inside her. Finally, she sighed.

'Okay, I suppose it's only fair to tell you why I need the

money. It's for bribes so we can continue to stay in the house.'

'But I thought your uncle had a permit. Aren't you legally entitled to live there?'

'Not now.'

'Why? . . . Becky, what's happened?'

Becky's face suddenly started to twitch, as though the underlying network of nerves was beginning to come alive after a long numbness. She swung away sharply and went to the opposite end of the room where, keeping her back turned, she fumbled for a handkerchief and blew her nose loudly.

'My uncle's dead,' she said in a flat, emotionless voice.

Instinctively, Candy moved towards her, but Becky looked round unexpectedly and her eyes warned Candy to keep her distance.

'I'm so sorry, Becky. I know it doesn't help, but . . .'

'He didn't do anything. He never hurt anybody in his whole life.'

Candy nodded dumbly, as Becky repeated more wildly, 'He didn't do anything. There was fighting in the street; some *tsotsis* ran into the shop – he had locked the door, but they broke it down – and they started grabbing everything. When he tried to stop them, they stabbed him.'

'I'm so sorry,' Candy said again uselessly.

Becky looked at her as if she had temporarily forgotten who she was talking to.

'I'm going now,' she said curtly after a moment. 'Thank you for the money.'

'Just a sec . . . I still don't understand why . . . I mean, well, couldn't your other uncle get a permit for the house?'

'No!' Becky said from the doorway. 'He doesn't qualify under Section Ten.'

'Oh hell! . . . I see.'

'You don't. You don't see anything. How could you?' Becky gestured angrily round the room. '*Your* policemen protect you, shoot people – unarmed children, so you can sit there seeing nothing you don't want to. But they can't shoot all of us, we're too many. And one day . . .' She gave a defiant shrug, and then looked Candy straight in the eye, calmly.

Candy looked back at her, feeling hollow inside, without defence or subterfuge. As they faced each other in silence, something strange happened: the barriers between them seemed to dissolve suddenly, and intuitively they recognized in the transparency of the moment that they were still friends. Whatever else they had lost, they had not lost their liking for each other. Involuntarily, they both began to smile at the same time.

Then Becky shook her head slightly, as if trying to clear some inner confusion, and said coolly, 'So? Now do you want me to give you back this seven rand, and forget about the rest of the loan?'

'Of course not. Don't be crazy,' Candy told her. 'I'll pay it off as soon as I can.'

'Becky . . . How about paying me back by giving me Zulu lessons? – the ones we never started.'

'You still want to learn Zulu?' Becky sounded both surprised and sarcastic.

'Yes.'

'Okay. We can start on Sunday. But this time we'll work – no messing about. Okay?'

'Okay.'

'I'll prepare something. See you then.'

'What about . . .' Candy started to say, but Becky had already gone.

A little while later Candy's mother came into the room and found Candy sprawled on the bed, her face buried in a pillow.

'Is anything the matter, dear?' she asked softly.

Candy tried to breathe normally in the hope that her mother would think she was asleep and go away. However, her mother obviously wasn't fooled because she settled herself at the foot of the bed and said in a worried, gentle voice, 'Becky didn't stay long. Is she all right?'

Candy mumbled something and pulled the pillow further over her head to hide the fact that she was crying.

After a long pause, her mother said, 'What did she have to say? . . . It is Becky, isn't it? She's upset you for some reason. What is it? If I don't know, I can't try to help.'

'Try . . . to . . . help?' Candy coughed, and then her nose started running. She rolled over on to her stomach and felt under the sheet for her tissue. Her mother leaned forward and gave her a clean one.

'I'm sorry, dear, I didn't catch what you said.'

'I don't want to talk about it.'

'Well . . . Is there anything I can do?'

Candy smiled bitterly. 'Not now,' she said. 'It's a bit late, isn't it?'

'What do you mean, dear?'

'Hell, Mum, all this time you've gone out of your way to avoid any mention of Becky – you haven't wanted to know a single damn thing about her. And now, all of a sudden . . .' Candy's voice broke. Clenching her teeth in an effort to control her trembling, she sat up and rubbed her swollen eyelids.

Her mother was completely still and silent. When Candy glanced at her from under her arm, she saw that she wasn't angry, merely sad and looking suddenly worn out. Faint wrinkles, resembling small bloodless scratches, marked her cheeks, and her normally bright blue eyes seemed faded, fatigue showing in them clearly like dark bruises.

'I don't think that's quite fair,' her mother said finally. 'But let's not argue about it. I like Becky – I told you I did. And I'm sorry if I've given you the impression that I don't care. I do. However, what you still don't seem to understand is . . .'

'I do understand,' Candy told her. 'I understand only too

well. Ignorance is bliss, knowledge is guilt. And we're afraid
– scared stiff, all of us. Becky's dead right, you know, we sit
here seeing nothing we don't want to.'

Her mother remained silent. After a while, Candy croaked,
'I don't blame her for despising me. God, when I think . . .'
She shrugged, fighting back her tears.

Her mother waited a moment, and then asked quietly,
'What did she have to say about the situation in Soweto?
Are her family all right? She looks half-starved.'

'All I know is that her uncle has been killed, and he was
like a father to her. And her family are about to be kicked
out of their house. That's why Becky came here – to ask me
if I would lend her money so they could try to bribe some
official to let them stay on in the house illegally.'

'Oh. You should have told me. How much did she want?'

'What difference does it make?' Candy said irascibly 'It's
my own money.' When her mother didn't reply, she continued, 'As a matter of fact, I'm giving her fifty rand – all the
money I've got left in the post office.'

Candy expected her mother to say something to that, but
she didn't. Her gaze remained fixed on the floor, a pensive
frown creasing her forehead.

'Becky's going to pay me back by continuing with my Zulu
lessons,' Candy offered in a friendlier tone.

Her mother nodded absently. 'Tell me some more about
her family. Doesn't she have a father?'

Slowly, almost grudgingly at first, Candy began to explain
all the facts of Becky's existence as she knew them. Apart
from asking the odd question, her mother made no comment
until she had finished.

'Becky's a bright kid, isn't she,' her mother said then. 'It
would be a pity if she wasn't able to complete her education.
Perhaps we could help by taking on the cost of her schooling.'

Candy was doubtful. 'I don't know. I'm not sure she'll
accept any help. She told me she didn't want charity from me.'

'We'll have to see. There must be some way of arranging it, maybe even anonymously if that's possible. I'll speak to Dad about it tonight. Becky's coming this Sunday, you say?'

'Yes.'

'Well, I'd better think of something nourishing to make for tea. And you see to it that she eats this time. We can't have her going about like a bag of bones any longer. Now can we?' her mother added defensively as Candy smiled at her.

'No,' Candy agreed, beginning to laugh.

'What's so funny then?' her mother demanded.

'You,' Candy told her, but she said it affectionately, and after a moment her mother also began to laugh.

'You're looking a bit chirpier now anyway,' her mother commented, looking happier herself, and also younger again as her eyes lit up suddenly. 'Do you know,' she said, 'I almost forgot to tell you – guess who rang this morning?'

Candy shrugged. She wasn't in the mood for guessing.

'Your favourite uncle.'

'Uncle Jack?' Candy's interest quickened. 'What did he have to say?'

'He and Pam are coming out here in October. Isn't that marvellous news?'

'They'll be staying with us, I hope?'

'I'm afraid not. Of course, Jack knows they're very welcome to, but as they'll be here for several months – apparently Jack has some long leave – he thinks it will be better if I find them a flat to rent in the neighbourhood. He still has a lot of friends in Johannesburg, you know, and he loves entertaining. I can see that they'll need their own space and privacy and independence for the length of visit they're planning.'

'Will they be here for Christmas?'

'Yes.' Her mother's smile widened. 'We'll have a big family celebration – just like old times.'

150

Candy groaned. 'Surely you're not going to invite all the old fogeys?'

Her mother laughed. 'Old fogeys indeed. Don't let Dad hear you talking like that. Naturally, everybody must be included. They'll all be dying to meet Pam. You know, I never thought Jack would settle down and get married. He didn't seem the marrying type somehow.'

'I only hope she's nice,' Candy muttered.

'I'm sure she is, dear. She sounds an absolute love from her letters.'

'So long as she doesn't talk with a hot potato in her mouth.'

'Candy! What's the matter with you? I thought you'd be thrilled by the news.'

'I am,' Candy said. But she was thinking that six years was a long time. She had changed; Uncle Jack must have changed; she was afraid of being disappointed when she met him again. And anyway, thinking about her own uncle had made her think of Becky's. 'He is a very good man,' Becky had said at their first meeting.

He never hurt anybody in his whole life . . .

'Why don't you get washed and come and have some tea,' her mother was saying. 'It's all ready in the lounge. I could make you a cup of coffee if you like?'

Candy shook her head, but she got up and followed her mother out of the room. 'Do you believe in reincarnation?' she asked as they went down the passage.

Her mother stopped in surprise. 'What an odd question,' she said. 'What makes you ask that now?'

'Well, do you?'

Her mother gave a little laugh. 'I don't know. I've never really thought about it. Why? Do you?'

'There's *got* to be some meaning to it all somewhere,' Candy said desperately, and she turned and went back up the passage, leaving her mother staring after her with a look of worried bewilderment on her face.

Becky arrived promptly at three the following Sunday, and immediately began unpacking her satchel – the one Candy had bought her months back.

'I've written out a list of vocabulary and a few simple sentences to start with,' she said in a brisk, business-like manner. 'Now, if you'll just clear some space on your desk . . .'

'Aren't we going to have tea first?' Candy asked hopefully, indicating the loaded tray at her elbow.

'We can have it as we work.' Becky pushed an open exercise book, the first page of which was filled with her clear, neat printing, in front of Candy. 'I'll say each word slowly, and you repeat it after me. Right?'

'Yes, ma'am,' Candy smiled.

'This is no time to be funny,' Becky snapped, and she turned her back to rummage in the satchel for a pencil.

Candy sighed inwardly and set her mind to the task in hand. However, as the lesson progressed, she found herself becoming increasingly irritated by Becky's unyielding attitude, and the humourless, almost contemptuous tone in which Becky corrected her mispronunciation and answered her questions. But she managed to stop herself from saying anything in the hope Becky would come round, given time.

After an hour, however, Candy had had enough.

'*Ubona-ni ?* -- What do you see?' Becky asked her.

'*Ngibona inja* – I see a dog,' Candy told her grumpily. 'Could we leave it at that now? I'm tired.'

'All right.' Becky closed the book. 'You must practise what we've done during the week. Next Sunday we'll concentrate on grammar. But to begin with, I wanted you to get the taste of the music of Zulu on your tongue. The – what's it called again? – the intonation is very important.'

'It's a beautiful language, but its construction is a lot more complicated than I thought it would be.'

'So? . . .' Becky's voice cracked like ice. 'You mean we've

just come out of the jungle so our language ought to be very simple – just a series of grunts maybe.'

Candy felt she had reached the end of her tether. 'No, of course not,' she said angrily. 'I didn't . . .'

But Becky wouldn't let her finish. 'That's the trouble with you whites,' she sneered. 'You're all the same underneath – the whole stinking lot of you. You call yourselves human? – you don't know the first thing about being human. *You* . . .' She jabbed her finger viciously at Candy. '*You* make me sick, you know that? So sick I could . . .'

'Is that so?' Candy jumped up, knocking over her chair. 'Well, let me tell you that . . .'

'Tell *me*?' Becky shouted. '*You* can't tell *me* anything. I'll tell you something. You know what's wrong with you? You're . . .'

'Will you shut up a . . .' Candy yelled, and then Becky struck her hard across the face.

The sound of the slap seemed to echo endlessly in the hush that followed. Candy was too stunned to feel anything, even the pain of the blow.

Becky was the first to break the silence. 'I shouldn't have done that,' she said. 'But I won't be told to shut up by anybody any more.'

Candy nodded as she lowered herself on to the edge of the desk. Sensation was coming back. Automatically, she raised her hand and covered her burning cheek.

'Are you all right?' Becky asked anxiously. 'I didn't mean to hit you so hard.'

A little weakly, Candy started to laugh. For some reason, Becky's assurance seemed ridiculously funny.

Becky looked at her as if she was afraid she had taken leave of her senses. 'Are you okay? . . . Candy? . . .'

'I'm fine,' Candy gulped. 'Don't worry.' She was laughing uncontrollably now.

After a moment, Becky grinned foolishly. 'I'm very sorry anyway,' she said.

Her words made Candy remember her dream and she stopped laughing. 'I'd much rather you slapped me than shot me,' she said wryly, and was about to explain further when she noticed Becky was no longer grinning and there were tears in her eyes. In silence, Candy put an arm round her. Becky let her hold her, saying nothing.

There was a sudden movement in the doorway. Candy looked up in time to catch a glimpse of her mother tiptoeing silently away. She must have come to find out what all the shouting was about, Candy realized, and felt thankful that her mother had been sufficiently sensitive not to intrude.

Eventually, Becky raised her face and smiled faintly. 'I've had enough of crying,' she said.

'It's your uncle, isn't it?' Candy asked gently.

Becky shrugged. 'Hey, your cheek looks awful. It's gone all red. Hadn't we better put some cold water on it or something?'

'Don't worry about it. It's not even hurting any more.'

'He never once hit anybody, you know,' Becky said unexpectedly, with fierce emotion. 'Never once in his whole life, not even when he was a boy – my mother told me. He hated violence of any sort.'

'He must have been a very special person.'

'He never lost his temper either. He was always kind and gentle, and funny. He used to laugh a lot, make jokes all the time. Everybody loved him.'

A lump was forming in Candy's throat. 'I wish I could have met him,' she said gruffly.

'Maybe he was too kind, I don't know.' Becky turned and picked up her pencil off the desk. She began to play with it, rolling it back and forth between her hands, and then stabbing the point repeatedly into her palm.

'Why do you say that?' Candy asked after a while.

Becky gave a short, painful laugh. 'He was no good at business, I can tell you,' she said, as if she hadn't heard the

154

question. 'He could have made money in the shop, but he was always poor. My aunt used to get very cross with him sometimes because he let people have things on credit when he knew they wouldn't ever be able to pay him. She kept telling him he was stupid, but he just used to smile and say, "How can I let very poor people starve when I've got food in my shop?" My aunt said he had no right to take food out of our mouths. We never went hungry though. So . . .'

For a few moments, Becky stood unmoving, her face half-turned away from Candy. Then she looked round and grinned apologetically.

'What's the time?' she asked.

'My watch is fast, but I think it's about half past four. You don't have to go yet, do you?'

'I must. I promised my mother I'd help her do some iron-ing this evening. She's trying to get money by taking in washing.'

'Oh. That reminds me.' Candy reached across the desk for the envelope with Becky's name on it. 'Here's the fifty rand. I hope it does the trick.'

'I'm not sure I ought to take it now,' Becky said.

'Why?'

'Well, look at your face,' Becky laughed uncomfortably.

Candy also laughed. 'You were right, you know – about what you said. I've got to tell you something.' She paused, blushing.

'You can't tell me anything,' said Becky, but her tone was self-mocking, and as they both laughed again – more freely this time, Candy found it easier to continue.

'It's been bothering me a lot,' she admitted. 'And yet I can't help it. It's just how I feel, even though it makes me a hypocrite. But I have to be honest about it, otherwise . . .'

'I know what you're going to say,' Becky cut in humor-ously. 'You don't like the way black people smell.'

However, Candy was too involved now in her own feelings,

to manage more than a complaisant smile. 'No,' she said, and went on awkwardly, in a sudden rush, 'I don't want a black government.'

'I see.' Becky nodded glumly.

'I feel guilty as hell about all the unjust inequalities between us. But when it really comes down to it, I don't know that I'd actually be prepared to commit myself to anything that could result in the loss of my own freedom. So you're right in thinking whatever you do about me.'

Becky studied her thoughtfully.

'You feel guilty as hell, yet you believe yourself to be free. Doesn't sound much like real freedom to me.'

Candy had to think about that. However, Becky didn't wait for an answer. 'Anyway, that's your problem,' she continued. 'That's the spook on your shoulder. I've got my own spook to worry about.'

'Yes?'

'Bitterness.' Becky spat the word out as if she was trying to expel its flavour from her mouth. 'I mustn't let it eat me up. I've seen what it does to people.' She sucked in air, making a whistling sound, and shook her head slowly. 'They become so full of hate in the end that they destroy themselves as human beings.'

Candy watched her as she began to gather her things together, too surprised by this new Becky to know what to say. The sullen schoolgirl of a short time ago seemed to have been transformed suddenly into a self-contained young woman, and Candy was left feeling less sure of herself and somewhat confused as to her own thinking.

When Becky was ready to go, Candy said impulsively, 'You know, I really wouldn't mind if you were prime minister.'

She had spoken seriously, but Becky started to laugh, and the old teasing brightness was back in her eyes. 'I'd give you a fair trial,' she promised. 'If you could conduct your own defence in good enough Zulu, I'd let you go free. Maybe I'd even appoint you Minister of Race Relations. We'd have to see.'

Candy smiled uncertainly.

'*Moenie* worry,' Becky told her, putting an arm round her shoulder. 'We shall try to overcome, somehow.'

'I hope so.'

'It's good to be honest with each other. I'm glad.'

'Me too.'

'It's the truth.' Becky raised her right fist in a black power salute. 'We swear to tell the truth, the whole truth, and . . .'

'Oh, get away with you,' Candy said, feeling more on top of herself again. 'Come on, I'll walk you to the bus stop.'

They had just started down the drive when Dirk turned in at the gateway on his scooter. Candy stopped in her tracks. She hadn't wanted Becky to meet Dirk yet; at least not until she had had a chance to talk to Becky about him.

'Who's that?' Becky nudged her arm. 'Your brother? Don't tell me I'm going to find out what he looks like at last.'

'No, it isn't Colin,' Candy said, reddening, as Dirk got off his scooter and began pushing it towards them.

'It must be your boyfriend then. Is it?'

Candy didn't answer. 'I thought you were supposed to be swotting this afternoon?' she called out accusingly to Dirk.

'*Ja*. But I got lonely.' He gave her an apologetic grin, before glancing at Becky.

'Oh well . . .' Candy shrugged, and introduced them to each other.

'*Sakubona*,'* Dirk said, shaking Becky's hand.

'You speak Zulu?' Becky asked him.

'Not really,' Dirk admitted. 'Candy taught me that. It's about the only word I know.'

'Candy did?' Becky was amused.

Candy said nothing. She was acutely conscious of Dirk's

* *hallo*

157

accent. Surely Becky must have realized by now that he was Afrikaans?

'Were you two going somewhere?' Dirk asked next.

'I'm taking Becky to the bus stop.'

'Can I give you a lift?'

'Don't be crazy,' said Candy. 'You can't fit three people on that thing.' Out of the corner of her eye, she was aware of Becky studying them both with quizzical interest.

'You want to bet?' Dirk laughed. 'Look, man, there's loads of room.'

Becky looked as directed, then started to smile at Dirk. 'What would we hold on to, to stop ourselves falling off?' she asked him in Afrikaans.

Dirk's face stiffened slightly. But Becky's smile seemed friendly enough, and after a moment he smiled back. 'You can hold on to me,' he told her.

Candy relaxed and began to enjoy the situation as Becky said, speaking English again now, 'And what happens if *you* fall off?'

'Then you hope like hell you fall on top of me. You needn't worry though, I don't fall off very often.'

Becky turned to Candy. 'I've never been on a scooter,' she said.

'We'll soon fix that,' said Dirk promptly. 'Hop on, both of you.'

Candy shook her head. 'Take Becky. I'll stay here. There isn't room for us all. And anyway, it's illegal. We might be stopped by the police . . . Go on. Don't be chicken,' she encouraged Becky, who was looking doubtful about the idea. 'You'll enjoy it, it's great fun. And it'll save time if you're in a hurry to get home.'

Dirk had already started the scooter. 'Come on then,' he urged Becky, patting the seat behind him.

'Okay,' Becky decided suddenly. 'But if the police see us, you know they might stop us anyway, and ask us what we're up to. You'd better say I'm your washgirl – or there could be trouble, I can tell you.'

'Hell, no, man.' Dirk grinned wickedly. 'I'll say we're just going to have it off in the veld.'

Candy didn't know how Becky would take that, but she merely laughed and climbed on to the scooter. Dirk winked at Candy.

'See you,' he said. 'Won't be long.'

He let out the clutch slowly, and the scooter began to move away more smoothly than usual. Candy watched them until they were out of sight, amused at Becky's clownish attempts to turn and wave while still holding on tightly at the same time.

She could hear them laughing as they went down the street, and the thought occurred to her that, under different circumstances, Dirk and Becky would have a great deal in common. 'I suppose I ought to be thankful for the Immorality Act,' she told herself with a heavy sense of irony.

Feeling a little overwhelmed by everything that had happened that afternoon, Candy went back to the veranda to wait for Dirk's return.

'What took you so long?' she complained when he finally appeared. 'I was starting to get worried.'

Dirk eased himself on to the settee beside her. '*Ag*, you know, I thought I'd better just stick around and make sure Becky got on her bus.'

'And did she?'

'*Ja.*'

Candy gave him a suspicious look. 'You seem very pleased with yourself,' she remarked. 'Why are you grinning like that?'

Instead of answering, Dirk leaned forward and kissed her on the tip of her nose.

'Hey! What's this?' he asked suddenly. Candy winced as he touched her cheek.

159

'It's nothing . . . I hit my face on the corner of my desk when I was bending down to pick up something. I didn't know it had left a mark. Is it very red?'

'Not very. But you're lucky you didn't get a black eye.'

'Anyway, I'm glad you've finally met Becky,' Candy said, changing the subject. 'Now that she knows you, I can ask her if it's all right for you to join the Zulu lessons – that's if you still want to?'

'*Ja*, I do.' Dirk rubbed the back of his hair a few times. 'To tell you the truth . . .' he paused, looking sheepish. 'I've already asked her. I hope you don't mind?'

Candy was astonished. 'What did she say?'

'It's okay with her . . . Do you mind?'

'No . . . No, of course not. I'm just surprised that she . . . Well, I was worried about her meeting you because . . . Oh hell, forget it. I'm just very glad the two of you liked each other.'

Dirk was laughing at her embarrassment. Candy shoved him playfully. 'Damn you. I suppose you realize I'm going to have to work hard now at my Zulu, so as not to be shown up.'

'You are,' Dirk promised, and he put an arm round her.

They were both silent for a while. Then Candy said quietly, 'Don't you think Becky is very attractive?' She had closed her eyes, resting her head on Dirk's shoulder.

'She is, *ja*.'

When Candy opened her eyes, Dirk was looking down at her, his face in shadow with the sun behind him.

'Did you know that you've got the most beautiful blue eyes?' he told her after a moment.

Candy realized she had been needing him to say something like that. 'My nose is too long though,' she mumbled.

'It's not. It's just right. It's a lovely nose.' He ran his finger lightly along the top of it.

'You know what I'd like to do now?' Candy said. She had decided it was a day for new resolutions.

160

'Mhhmm!' Dirk was nuzzling her ear. 'Me too. Why don't we?'

'Stop it. I'm being serious.' She pushed him back a little, afraid of the way her body was responding to the teasing quality of his caresses.

'So am I,' Dirk assured her. But he released her with an exaggerated sigh of resignation, and folded his arms, waiting for her to speak.

'I'd like to go over to your house and have some coffee, and listen to you reading Afrikaans poetry.'

Dirk stared at her in amazement. 'Is that what you really want to do?'

'Yes,' Candy said firmly.

'Hell, I don't know, man. I don't think I've got any poems in translation.'

'I don't want you to read them to me in English, you goof. I want to hear them in Afrikaans.'

'*Ja?* . . . Would you understand enough?'

Candy reddened. 'Whatever I don't understand, you can explain.' She stood up. 'So? . . . Are we going, or aren't we?'

Dirk also stood up, more slowly. 'I don't read very well,' he warned.

'I'll be my own judge of that,' Candy told him briskly.

8

Becky had changed. She didn't talk much about her experiences during the recent troubled months, but on the edge of bitterness she had obviously gained a firmer resolve and self-belief.

'If I've learned only one thing from what's been happening in Soweto,' she told Candy, 'it's that I have a right to be respected as a human being.'

Her new self-assurance was immediately apparent in the way she related to Candy's parents. To Candy's surprise, Becky accepted their offer to finance her education without hesitation, and discussed the details with Candy's mother in a calmly grateful manner that lacked any hint of humbleness or embarrassment. It was Candy's mother who was embarrassed, blushing and stammering in her eagerness to convince Becky that the offer did not place her under any obligation.

Becky made a point of seeking out Candy's father to thank him as well, approaching him without any trace of her former shyness. Candy had to hide a smile at seeing her father become gruff and red-faced, clearly uncertain how to react to this confident young black woman who smiled straight into his eyes in friendly defiance of his white status and authority.

'You amaze me, you know,' Candy told Becky afterwards, when they were walking to the bus stop.

'Why?' Becky asked.

The slight sharpness in her voice made Candy hesitate, afraid of being misunderstood. 'I don't know,' she said evasively. 'You just do.'

'I can guess what you're thinking. You think it's funny I'm not too proud to take money from your parents. Right?'

'No, it's not . . . Look, don't get me wrong, I . . .'

'There's a lot you don't understand,' Becky interrupted her, quietly but forcefully. 'The only thing that matters to me right now is that I complete my education. Even if it is only Bantu Education' – she stressed the last two words sarcastically. 'It's still better than nothing. I've got to go on learning, developing my mind. I've got to. I've got to have as much knowledge as possible, even if I have to starve to get it.' She stopped walking and grabbed Candy's arm. 'You want to know why?'

Candy nodded nervously, wondering what she was leading up to. Becky's eyes had become feverishly bright, although the rest of her face remained calm and composed.

'It's no use fighting for your freedom if you don't know how to use it constructively and wisely when you get it. And I don't mean knowing how to make yourself fat and wealthy. I mean knowing how to try to make sure everybody gets a fair deal. Hitlers come in all colours, I can tell you.' Becky shook her head. 'Too many people still can't think for themselves. How can they choose the right leaders when they can't even read and write? They need to be educated about a lot of things. I want to be of some use when the time comes. But I can't help anybody until I know enough myself.'

They were facing each other, only inches apart. The shining intensity of Becky's eyes seemed to burn through Candy like a laser beam. All the old fears loomed up in her mind.

'Becky . . .' Candy glanced around almost furtively to make certain there wasn't anyone else within hearing. 'Becky, listen . . . Of course you don't have to answer this if you don't want to. But . . . Well, are you involved in anything subversive?'

Becky stared at her, and then slowly started to smile. 'Depends what you mean by "subversive". If you mean, do I belong to an underground organization, then I can tell you, no. But from what I've been saying to you, you could call me subversive, I suppose.' Her smile widened into a teasing grin. 'Why? You planning to turn me over to BOSS*?'

Candy blushed, suddenly uncomfortably aware of the extent to which her fear had made her reluctant to listen to what Becky was trying to tell her.

Becoming serious again, Becky went on, 'I can tell you, I support all the aims of the Black Consciousness movement. Do you know about it?'

'I've heard of it, but I don't know much about it,' Candy admitted.

'For a start, black people have got to realize their own worth. We've got to stop letting ourselves be made to feel inferior. Know what I mean? . . . Black is beautiful, man.' The grin was back on Becky's face. 'But white's okay too. I'm not a racialist.'

Candy gave a shaky laugh 'I'm glad about that.'

'Anyway,' Becky shrugged. '. . . What the hell are we doing standing talking like this on the street corner. You want us to get arrested under the Riotous Assemblies Act? Come on, I've got a bus to catch.'

After they had been walking for a few minutes, Candy asked, 'What's it like in Soweto now? I worry about you having to get home from the station. It must be even more dangerous at the moment to wander about on your own.'

Becky merely laughed.

'What about your family? Are they all okay?'

'We're all okay,' Becky assured her, smiling.

'And the house? Did you get the permit business sorted out?'

'We're all okay for now,' Becky repeated. 'For today, we're all right. I can't tell you for tomorrow. When you live in Soweto, you have to live from day to day, that's all.'

'Becky,' Candy said with a note of desperation in her voice. 'What do you think is going to happen?'

* Bureau of State Security

'I don't know.' Becky glanced at her. 'What do you mean? Do you mean what's going to happen in Soweto?'

'I suppose so.' Candy wasn't sure exactly what she had meant.

'People are very angry, I can tell you. They're not going to give up easily. You know, they've been burning down schools and other government buildings. I can understand why they want to do it. But I don't think it helps to burn down schools.' A cynical, almost self-mocking grin lifted the corners of her lips as she added, 'I hope they don't burn down my school. I've got to get my matric so I can study further.'

Candy suddenly shot out her arm and stopped Becky in mid-stride. 'Hold on a sec,' she cried excitedly. 'I've just had an idea. Perhaps you could get a scholarship to study overseas – once you've got your matric. I'm sure some British universities, for instance, provide grants for foreign students. It could be fantastic, don't you think?'

'Why?'

Carried away by her own enthusiasm, Candy failed to notice the coolness in Becky's tone. 'Well, jeepers! You'd learn so much more, and you'd be free to do what you liked.'

Becky regarded her through narrowed eyelids, with her mouth pulled in tightly.

'I don't want to be free anywhere else,' she said fiercely. 'I want to be free in my own country,' and she swung round sharply and began to walk on.

After that, neither of them spoke again until they had reached the main road. Then Becky said, 'I want to tell you that I wouldn't accept money from your mother if I didn't like her. I like her very much. I always have.'

'Sure,' said Candy.

Becky thought for a moment. 'I like your father too,' she decided. And suddenly she was grinning again. 'He doesn't say much though, does he?'

'No.' Candy laughed. 'To be honest, I don't think he

quite knew how to react to you. You've changed a lot, you know.'

'It's the truth,' Becky agreed. 'But then so have you.'

They smiled warmly at each other.

'Will you promise me one thing, Becky?' Candy asked half-seriously. 'Don't ever lose your sense of humour or I'll lose my faith in the human spirit.'

'What's that supposed to mean?'

'Forget it. I don't want to give you a swollen head. There's your bus – you'd better run.'

'Like a rabbit. See you next Sunday, and make sure you've learned that list of vocabulary . . . Hey! The Giraffe's starting then, isn't he?'

Candy nodded.

'Well, tell him I won't have any loafers in my class. And give him my love.'

'I'm not sure I'll do that,' Candy replied, laughing. But Becky was already racing towards the bus stop and gave no sign of having heard.

*   *   *

One Sunday afternoon in early October, Candy, Dirk and Becky were sprawled on Candy's bed, relaxing after a Zulu lesson, when there was a timid knock on the door.

'Come in,' Candy called, thinking it must be her mother come to fetch the tea tray.

However, it was Elaine's face which appeared round the edge of the door. 'I hope we're not disturbing you?' she said. 'But we heard you laughing so we thought the lesson must be over. Do you mind if we come and join you?'

'By all means. The more the merrier.' Candy beckoned her in, wondering who was with her. It seemed highly unlikely that it would be Colin.

But it was. He sauntered into the room a few steps behind Elaine, and shrugged at Candy as if to indicate that this hadn't been his idea.

166

Candy gave him a warning look to behave himself or he'd be sorry, and stood up to introduce Becky to both of them.

'So you're the phantom brother,' Becky said, grinning at Colin. 'I was beginning to believe you didn't exist.'

'Oh, I exist all right,' Colin told her bluntly, and immediately turned to talk to Dirk.

'Come on, Dirk,' Candy said hurriedly. 'Shove up, will you, so we can all fit on the bed.'

With a grateful smile, Elaine squeezed herself into the space next to Becky and began chatting to her. Finding himself standing alone, Colin hesitated for a moment, and then fetched himself a chair from the other side of the room.

He lounged back with his hands in his pockets and his legs crossed, looking bored and making no attempt to join in the conversation. However, Candy noticed that although he appeared to be totally uninterested in anything going on around him, every now and then he glanced surreptitiously in Becky's direction. And whenever he did so, a strange look – almost of fear – crossed his face. Puzzled, Candy began to watch him closely out of the corner of her eye.

After a while Becky looked up, and catching him staring at her, grinned back. Colin instantly averted his eyes and pretended to be studying the calendar hanging on the wall behind her. But he had gone bright red. And suddenly, Candy remembered a long-forgotten incident from childhood.

She couldn't have been more than nine – which meant Colin would have been eleven, or had perhaps turned twelve – when she had walked into his bedroom to find him lying on the bed, staring intently at the photograph of a buxom black girl decorating the front cover of a magazine.

'What you doing, Colly?' she had asked.

'Nothing. I'm busy. Go away.'

Wanting to be sociable, she had said, 'You think she's pretty?' stabbing a small finger at the face in the photograph.

'You must be crazy.' But he had blushed scarlet.

'You do,' she had insisted with the undiplomatic directness of the very young.

'I do *not*, dammit!'

'You do.'

'I bloody don't. How bloody could I? She's bloody black. Now get out of here. I told you I'm busy.'

'You do though,' she had taunted, aware of the effect she was having, and wanting to pay him back for rejecting her friendly approach.

'Get out of here,' he had shouted at her in a sudden rage. 'If you don't bugger off this bloody instant I'll clobber you, d'ye hear?'

She had heard and had left quickly, knowing he wouldn't hesitate to carry out his threat.

'So that's it,' Candy thought now. 'Of course. How stupid of me not to have realized before.' Evidently, Colin was attracted to black women, but was afraid to acknowledge his feelings, believing them to be unnatural. That explained the compulsive and yet oddly fearful way in which he kept looking at Becky. 'Becky must really disturb him,' Candy thought to herself.

Within the past few months, Becky's adolescent attractiveness seemed to have blossomed in a striking way. She had put on a little weight, and had discarded the old, somewhat childish style of cotton skirts and dresses in preference for jeans and brightly coloured T-shirts, which showed off her slim figure to much better advantage. The hollows in her cheeks had also filled out, giving her face a rounded smoothness within its basic heart-shaped structure.

Watching Becky as she sat laughing at Elaine's comical attempts to pronounce the three click sounds in Zulu, Candy decided that only a blindly prejudiced person could fail to find her extremely attractive.

'It's no good,' Elaine wailed. 'I just can't do the "q" click at all. I think I must have a deformed tongue. Show me again what you're supposed to do.'

'Don't you worry,' Becky encouraged her. 'You've nearly got it. Look, you press the front of your tongue – like this, see? – against the top of your mouth here . . . and then you release it sharply – so.' She demonstrated.

'No, it's no use,' Elaine said, giggling. 'I can't make it sound like that.'

'But it's easy,' Dirk teased her.

'I wouldn't boast if I were you,' Becky told him. 'When you started, you sounded like a frog with bellyache.'

'It's the truth,' Candy agreed.

Becky just gave her a look, and turned back to Elaine. 'You're doing fine,' she said. 'You're doing much better than they did to begin with, I can tell you. Try it again, and remember, you must let your tongue go sharply.'

However, Elaine laughed and shook her head. 'I'll practise in private,' she decided. Then she glanced across at Colin. 'What about you, Col? Why don't you have a try?'

The others all looked at Colin as if they had forgotten he was still there. Candy saw his eyes flicker towards Becky before he shifted irritably in his chair.

'Not me,' he said abruptly, and he frowned at Elaine. 'Do you realize what the time is? We'd better get a move on or we're going to be late.'

'We won't be. There's bags of time yet.' But she also made a move to get up. 'Before we go . . .' She turned and smiled at the other three. 'I wanted to invite you all to come and have a swim at my house next Sunday. Either before or after the Zulu lesson – whichever you prefer.' When none of them replied immediately, she looked pointedly at Candy.

'Well . . .' Candy hesitated, glancing at Becky. She felt the answer largely depended on her.

Becky grinned. 'Could be nice,' she said to Elaine. 'I haven't had a swim for a long time.'

'Good.' Elaine sounded relieved. 'That's a date then. Of course,' she went on with a persuasive smile, 'if you all felt like a holiday from the lessons, you could come for lunch and stay for the whole afternoon.'

Candy glanced once more at Becky. 'I don't know,' she said. 'It's up to the teacher. She's the boss.'

'I think I deserve a day off from teaching you two,' Becky told her. 'So it's okay by me.'

'Great! I'll expect you all at about one then. I only hope it's a nice day so we can have lunch round the pool.'

Candy nodded doubtfully. She was beginning to feel bothered about how Elaine's parents were going to react to the visit. But she found it difficult to believe that Elaine wouldn't have had the sense to consult them first.

'Colin can give you all a lift over,' Elaine continued. 'You'll be able to borrow your dad's car, won't you, Col?'

'What? . . . Oh yes, I suppose so,' Colin said ungraciously.

Becky dug Candy lightly in the ribs. 'There's just one problem, you know.'

'What's that?' Candy asked apprehensively.

'I don't have a swimming costume.'

'Don't worry, I can . . .' Candy began, but Dirk beat her to it.

'That's no problem,' he assured Becky with a grin. 'I've got a spare pair of trunks. You'll look really good in them.'

For the first time Colin actually laughed.

*　　*　　*

The visit to Elaine's house seemed to be a great success. Everybody appeared to enjoy themselves, and Elaine's parents went out of their way to make Becky feel welcome. Even Colin managed to be agreeable, and towards the end of the afternoon was actually beginning to talk to Becky directly.

Nevertheless, some lingering worry made Candy bring up the subject as soon as she and Becky were left alone together after the lesson the following Sunday – Dirk having been dragged away by Colin to inspect a car which Colin hoped to buy.

'So, did you enjoy the social gathering last week?' Candy asked straight off.

Becky's eyes studied her for a moment. 'Yes,' she said cautiously. 'They're nice people. Did you?'

Candy nodded. 'I like Elaine's parents. I find them easy to talk to.'

'Uh-huh.' Becky settled herself back more comfortably on the bed. She went on looking at Candy thoughtfully. 'They're very hospitable, that's for sure.'

Candy was about to agree when something in Becky's expression stopped her. Instead, she found herself asking, 'What do you mean?'

There was a pause. Becky began to smile gently, almost apologetically, as if she was trying to find a way of being honest without hurting. Candy's heart sank. She had a feeling she already knew what Becky was going to say.

'They treated me like a filmstar, you know,' Becky finally admitted.

She waited to see if Candy would comment, and then added with an embarrassed laugh, 'I don't suppose they've had an African visitor to their house before?'

In silence, Candy got up and went to the window. Staring out at the garden, she said, 'You *didn't* enjoy yourself then?'

'I didn't say that. I did enjoy myself. I like them. I already told you, I think they're very nice people. Very kind. It's not their fault. I'm not blaming them. But if you don't know what I mean, it doesn't matter.'

Candy bit back her angry retort. She couldn't really blame Becky for being honest, and for forcing her to face the truth. Suddenly feeling overcome by a general sense of weariness, she returned to the bed and sat down without looking at Becky.

'You know,' she said, 'I almost began to believe things were starting to be different. That we would be able to start going out and having fun together, instead of always having to stay shut up in this damn, bloody room.'

'Maybe they are – I mean maybe we will be able to,' Becky said encouragingly. 'Maybe what's been happening in Soweto will have some effect . . . I don't know. But anyway, we can always go and have a swim at Elaine's house again. Elaine said so. And her parents invited us too, remember?'

'But what's the point if . . .'

'It'll be better next time,' Becky assured her firmly. 'Next time won't be the first time. Everybody will be more natural and relaxed.'

However, Candy looked unconvinced. And then Becky burst out laughing.

'What's so funny all of a sudden?'

'I was thinking . . . Did you notice Elaine's mother offered me the same piece of cake four times at tea? . . . It's the truth. I was already full up to my ears, but in the end I took it just to make her happy.'

'I'm sorry,' Candy muttered. She felt too depressed to share Becky's amusement.

'Don't be crazy. What you saying sorry for? I can tell you, the same thing would happen if you came to see me in Soweto and I took you to visit some of my friends or relations. They would all rush round, making you sit in their best chair and giving you their best cup, to show you that *they* weren't prejudiced, and also to show you that they didn't hold any grudge against you personally for the way they had to live.'

'Damnation!' With an angry, despairing gesture, Candy stood up and crossed the room to stand in front of the window again.

It was a beautiful, warm, sunny afternoon outside. All the colours in the garden had a brilliance that hurt the eye. The soft, hissing spray from the hose sprinkler formed a fountain of sparkling silver specks which seemed to be suspended in the air above the rose bushes. Through the open window, Candy could smell the moist scent of the roses: a light, heady freshness that was mysteriously provocative, aggravating her restlessness. When she turned back into the room, the air inside seemed all the more stifling by comparison.

'God! If only we could get out of this bloody country for a bit. Even if it was just for a short while.'

Becky smiled up at her calmly. 'Where would you like to go?'

'I don't care. Anywhere where there wasn't apartheid.'

'You'd better start building a space ship then,' Becky remarked wryly.

'Damn it, you know what I mean. I want to go somewhere where we could at least *do* things together. Hell, if we could just get away from all this for a while, even if it was only for a month – or even a couple of weeks would help.'

'You *are* in a bad way.'

'Oh, well . . .' Candy sighed morosely. 'It's impossible, so . . .'

'It needn't be,' Becky said, suddenly resolute. 'I know somewhere we could go that's not too far.'

'Where?'

'Swaziland. I've got relations near Mbabane. If you like, I'm sure we could go and stay with them.'

Candy gave her a distrustful look. 'Are you being serious now? You're not having me on?'

'When do I ever tell you a lie? Of course I'm serious. We could go in the Christmas holidays. My relations won't mind. And they're really nice. I know you'll like them. I went to visit them once before with my mother, when I was very small. We had a lovely time there.'

Candy's face was beginning to brighten. 'How would we get to Mbabane?'

'By train. We'd have to travel separately, you know.'

'I don't care.' Candy wasn't going to let a small thing like that put her off. 'Swaziland. Wow! But are you sure your relations wouldn't mind us staying with them?'

'They'll be very happy. I'd better warn you though, it won't be the same as staying in the President Hotel. My relations aren't rich. They're not starving, but you'd have to get used to living quite basically. Nothing like this,' Becky added, looking round the room.

'I don't care. I'll love it,' Candy enthused, and was a little put out when Becky laughed at her.

'I can tell you, you wouldn't love it so much if it was forever.'

Candy didn't reply. It had just occurred to her that she still had to get her parents' permission to make the journey.

Noticing her suddenly doubtful expression, Becky said, 'What's up? Is it the Giraffe? If you're bothered about leaving him, ask him too. I don't mind.'

'No! I'm not worried about leaving Dirk – at all.' And then Candy became embarrassed, aware that she had sounded more certain than she had intended. 'Well . . . The fact is,' she admitted sheepishly, 'I don't think it will be at all a bad thing if Dirk and I can't see each other for a couple of weeks or so.'

'Why?' Becky asked bluntly.

'Well . . . you know . .'

'No, I don't,' Becky said, grinning at her with unconcealed curiosity. 'Aren't you sure if you like him any more?'

'No, no, it's not that. . . . I just feel it wouldn't do us any harm to have a break . . . It's sort of been getting a bit too intense recently, if you know what I mean.'

'Aahh! You mean the Giraffe wants you to sleep with him and you don't want to?'

Candy reddened to the roots of her hair. 'It's not quite that simple,' she confessed, starting to laugh uncomfortably.

'Aahh!' Becky said again, also beginning to laugh and

shaking her head. 'Boys! Too much trouble boys – that's what my uncle always used to say, you know.'

'I know,' Candy told her gently. But when she checked Becky's face anxiously, she found no sign of the former shadows of grief in her eyes.

'If it's that bad,' Becky went on placidly, 'if you both want to, then what's stopping you?'

'It's not *that* bad,' Candy said hurriedly. 'Anyway, I don't really want to – not yet. I'm not ready. I don't want the responsibility and the complications. Besides, no matter what anybody says, there's always the risk of . . . of . . .' She was too embarrassed to go on.

'Yes,' Becky agreed. 'It's the truth. Well, I wouldn't worry. The Giraffe's not one of your plastic disposables. He'll keep.'

'I'm *not* worried,' Candy insisted loudly. 'I only mentioned it in the first place to explain that . . . Oh to hell with you,' she said, smiling as she saw the amused look on Becky's face. Candy pretended to throw a pillow at her, and then lay back, leaning on her elbow.

'So, we're going to Swaziland, are we?' she asked after a moment.

'If we can find enough money. I don't know how much the train fares will be. And we'll also have to find out what documents we need to get out of the country. That might be a problem – I don't know. I wouldn't get too excited too soon, if I were you. Not until we've found out more about it all.'

'I don't care how difficult it is. We're going,' Candy said in a determined voice. 'We're going to Swaziland, and just let anyone or anything try to stop us.'

'What about your parents? You don't think they'll object?'

'They'd better not. I don't see why they should. I'll speak to them about it this evening . . . They won't mind, I'm sure,' Candy added. But she was already starting to feel a lot less confident than she sounded.

* * *

Candy's nails pressed painfully into the palms of her hands as she watched her mother carefully counting the stitches on her knitting needle. At last, her mother looked up.

'But dear,' she said. 'I just don't see how we could possibly let you go rushing off to a foreign country, to stay with people we know absolutely nothing about and whose customs and way of life must be very different from our own.'

'Becky wouldn't invite me to stay with people who aren't perfectly decent and respectable – even if they don't live the same way as we do. Surely you know her well enough by now, Mum, to realize that?'

Her mother merely tightened her mouth, saying nothing while she consulted her knitting pattern. Candy glanced across the room at her father, who was sitting with his back towards her, muttering as he added up the household accounts. He didn't appear to be listening to the conversation, but Candy knew that he was. Her mother started knitting again more quickly, as if she was trying to make up for lost time.

'Anyway,' Candy went on, 'if you're worried because you don't know anything about Becky's relations, you can always talk to Becky about them. As I told you, she's been to stay with them before, so she can answer any questions you have.'

'That's not all there is to it, dear,' her mother said quietly.

'No? Then what else is worrying you?'

Her mother pushed the stitches of her knitting firmly back along the needle, as though she felt they might get in the way of what she had to say.

'I just think you're still too young to go rushing off on your own to a . . .'

'But I'm not going on my own,' Candy pointed out. 'Hell's bells, Mum, I'm . . .'

'All right, all right. There's no need to get angry,' her mother said in a placatory voice that had the opposite effect on Candy. 'I do realize you'd be going with Becky. But it doesn't make any difference as far as I'm concerned. I still think you're both too young to go dashing off alone together on holiday, especially somewhere we know so little about. No, I'm sorry, dear, but it would be highly irresponsible of us to let you go. You're only just sixteen, after all.'

'Last year I was only fifteen. But I wasn't too young then, was I, to go dashing off alone with Jane to stay with her uncle and aunt in Cape Town. You didn't know her uncle and aunt from Adam and Eve, but you let me go and stay with *them*.'

'Now Candy,' her mother began to smile in protest, 'for goodness sake, dear, you know that was quite different. We . . .'

'Yes, it was, wasn't it – quite different,' Candy sneered, without giving her mother time to finish. 'Jane's uncle and aunt were white, whereas Becky's relations are black. That makes the difference, doesn't it?'

The room was suddenly very quiet. Candy became aware that her father's back had stiffened although he remained sitting as before, bent forward over the table with a pen in his hand. An angry red flush was spreading across her mother's cheeks, but she didn't speak. After a while, she gave a long sigh, and dropped her knitting into her lap.

'You seem determined to make me out to be a racialist,' she said.

Candy shrugged, without replying. Her face had taken on a set, stubborn look as she glared down at her mother in a resentful, challenging way.

'Well,' her mother said eventually, 'if that's what you want to believe, I can't stop you.' She glanced briefly towards the other side of the room. 'Perhaps you'd better ask your father what he thinks. I've told you my feelings, but see what he has to say.'

'All right.' Candy knew that they both knew perfectly well

what her father would say. He would support her mother's decision. He always did in such cases – on a matter of principle, if nothing else. But Candy couldn't allow her mother to think she wasn't prepared to stand up to him as well. Clenching her hands tightly at her sides, she half turned to face him.

'Well, Dad . . .?'

There was no answer.

Her mother resumed her knitting. 'I'm afraid he's getting a little deaf, dear,' she said. 'You'll have to speak louder.'

Almost immediately, Candy's father flung his pen across the table, and swivelled round in his chair. One look at his expression was enough to convince Candy of the state of his temper.

'I am not deaf,' he roared, but he was looking at Candy, not her mother. 'It might help if I was. It's difficult enough trying to concentrate on these damned accounts without having to listen to this ridiculous argument. You heard what your mother said. She told you you're too young to go. And so you are. When you're older, you can do as you like. But while you're still under age, you'll just have to put up with our judgement on these matters.' He jerked off his glasses.

'Now is that clearly understood?' he demanded, scowling ferociously.

Candy felt afraid, but she forced herself to meet his eye. 'Yes, it is. But I don't accept . . .'

'*Be quiet!* I will not have you answering back. You've done enough of that for one night, as it is. You've had your answer. You can't go, and that's final. I don't want to hear any more about it. Anyway,' he added a little less fiercely, checking his watch, 'it's time you were in bed. So off you go and let me get on with these damn things in peace.'

Candy didn't move. 'I'm sorry, Dad, but whatever you say, I'm . . .' The rest of her sentence was drowned in the clatter of her father's chair being knocked over as he sprang to his feet.

'No buts, I said,' he shouted. 'Didn't you hear me? I told you to go to bed. Now go. At once! Go on!'

Candy was already on her way to the door. When she got there she paused for a moment to steel herself, and then turned round.

'I don't care what you say,' she declared in a wobbly, slightly hysterical voice. 'I'm going to Swaziland. I have to, and I'm going.' And she slammed the door and took to her heels down the passage before her father could recover and call her back.

9

With her finger poised on the bell, Candy hesitated. She could hear Uncle Jack moving around inside the flat, humming quietly to himself. When his blurred outline showed up briefly through the frosted glass of the front door, she shrank back against the wall.

It didn't seem fair to burst in on him with her problem when he had only just arrived from London. On the other hand, if she was going to ask him for help, it had to be soon. She had no idea how long it would take to apply for passports or whatever other documents might be needed to get into Swaziland – especially in Becky's case.

'Besides, I want to see him anyway,' Candy told herself to salve her conscience. 'And I know he'll be glad to see me.' It had been clear as soon as they greeted each other at the airport yesterday that six years of separation had made no difference to the bond between them.

Making up her mind suddenly, she stepped forward and gave the bell a firm push. Uncle Jack opened the door, put out his arms and swept her joyfully inside before she had time even to open her mouth.

'I hope you don't mind if we sit in the kitchen,' he said as he shepherded her along the short, narrow passage. 'Pam's asleep on the settee in the living-room and I'd rather not disturb her just yet.'

'Oh hell. I hope *I* haven't woken her up.'

'Don't worry. She's sleeping the sleep of the dead. Poor love. I think she's still recovering from the flight and the sudden change of climate.'

'I really like her, you know. I think she's terrific.'

Uncle Jack looked boyishly pleased. 'She is,' he agreed.

'Now you sit down while I make us some coffee.' He pulled out a chair for Candy at the table. 'The occasion really calls for champagne, but we haven't got any, and your mother would probably kill me if I sent you home tipsy.'

'She's not coming here this afternoon, is she?'

Uncle Jack glanced round from the sink where he was filling the kettle. 'No. Not as far as I know. She and your dad are going to call in later this evening. I hope you'll come with them.'

'Uh . . . I probably won't, if you don't mind.' Candy could feel her face beginning to grow hot.

Uncle Jack gave her another odd look. However, he didn't say anything as he spooned coffee into two cups, and then walked to the fridge and took out a bottle of milk. After searching through several cupboards, he found the sugar bowl and brought it across to the table. He remained standing, his hands resting on the back of a chair, and smiled down at her with his eyes. He had her mother's eyes, except that his were an even clearer blue.

'Something tells me,' he said slowly in a gentle, concerned voice, 'that all is not quite hunky-dory between you and your parents at the moment. Or am I simply imagining things?'

Candy grinned painfully. 'No . . . I'm afraid you're not. Actually, to tell you the truth, I'm not talking to them. Well, not *really* talking.'

'Oh dear. Since when?'

'Last Sunday. We had this row, you see . . . God, I don't know . . .' Suddenly afraid that she was going to cry, Candy jumped up and went to switch off the kettle. The last thing she wanted was to make Uncle Jack feel sorry for her.

Without turning round, she asked huskily, 'Do you still take milk in your coffee?'

'Yes, please.'

He came and stood beside her quietly. He didn't touch her,

or even look at her, but immediately Candy felt herself becoming calmer.

'I don't want to hurt them,' she said, speaking almost normally now. 'But going to Swaziland with Becky means more to me than anything else in my life at the moment. It's not just that I want to go. I feel I desperately need to go for a lot of reasons. It's terribly important to me. But they don't seem to understand that. They . . .'

'Hold on a minute. Who's Becky again? Is she the African friend you wrote and told me about? The one who lives in Soweto?'

'That's right.' Candy was about to say more when Uncle Jack took her arm.

'Let's go and sit down,' he suggested. 'It sounds rather complicated, so I think you'd better tell me what it's all about from the beginning.'

When she had finished explaining the whole story to him he was silent for a while.

Eventually he asked, 'You're absolutely determined to go then, are you? No matter what?'

'Absolutely.'

'What will you do? Just walk out of the house with your suitcase when the time comes?'

Candy glanced at him warily, but his bland expression gave her no indication of what he was thinking.

'If I have to,' she said, gritting her teeth and meeting his gaze head-on. 'They can't stop me.'

'They could, you know,' Uncle Jack pointed out in the same neutral voice. 'Don't forget, you're still under age.'

Candy started to say something, then thought better of it, and shrugged instead.

'I know,' she admitted. 'That's the beastly problem. I know they could lock me up in my bedroom, or send the police after me to fetch me back.' She paused before going on, 'I realize they could also make things difficult for Becky if they wanted to. They could stop paying for her schooling, for a start. And they could put the police on to her, I suppose . . . Don't worry.' She grimaced. 'I've thought about it all – a helluva lot. In fact, I haven't been able to think about anything else for the past few days.'

'In that case, is it really worth while to go ahead, regardless?'

Candy frowned, staring down at the table. When at last she glanced up, there was a look of anguish in her eyes.

'I can't see Mum and Dad doing any of those things,' she said. 'Can you? I mean, they're just not like that.' She shook her head slowly. 'I can't believe they'd take it out on Becky, or actually physically try to stop me from going when it came to it.' And then she added, with a sudden doubt in her voice, 'Do you think they would?'

Uncle Jack pursed his lips. 'No, I don't think they would,' he decided, and he almost smiled. 'They're not exactly the sort of parents who would chain you to the bedpost. However, they're bound to be deeply hurt and angry. And your mother will be terribly worried about you.'

'Yes, I know,' Candy mumbled wretchedly.

They were both silent.

'But their fears are irrational,' Candy spoke out suddenly. She sat up, tensing her shoulders. 'They won't admit it, but I think their concern for my safety is based on prejudice. That's why I can't accept their decision. I *know* I'll be perfectly all right staying with Becky's relations. I won't come to any harm. So I'm going. I *have* to go. I really do. It's that important to me.'

Uncle Jack continued to gaze at her mildly for a moment or two without speaking. Then all he said was, 'And what about money? How are you going to pay for the trip?'

'I'm going to sell my guitar. I've never learned to play it, and someone at school is interested in buying it. It's worth quite a lot, so it should just about cover all our expenses.'

'You seem to have got it all worked out,' Uncle Jack said, actually smiling now.

'Yes, except . . . Well, we still have to find out about passports. I'm worried that there might be problems for Becky. I'd hate her to get into any trouble, so I don't think she ought to do anything herself until we've discovered what's involved. But I haven't a clue how to set about finding out. And anyway, you know what government officials are like. I can't see them being very helpful if they're approached by a young schoolgirl. So . . .' Candy wriggled uncomfortably, avoiding Uncle Jack's eye. Before she could continue, he started to laugh.

'I had a feeling I was going to come into it somewhere,' he said.

Candy looked at him, red-faced. 'But please don't think that you – I mean I don't want . . .'

'More coffee?' he suggested, and without waiting for an answer, he picked up their cups and went away to the other side of the room.

Candy watched him uneasily, wishing he would say something, anything, that would give her a clue as to what he was thinking. She was beginning to feel she couldn't stand the suspense any longer, when he brought back their refilled cups and perched on the edge of the table.

'I can't remember,' he said, 'if you've already told me when you're planning to go to Swaziland.'

'In December. As soon as possible after school breaks up.'

'And for how long?'

'A week, maybe two.'

'Really?' Uncle Jack stirred sugar into his coffee. 'What a strange coincidence. You see, Pam and I have been thinking about having a holiday in Swaziland at roughly the same time. I used to know a snazzy hotel with a swimming pool, not far from Mbabane. It's the ideal place in which to spend a relaxing week – or maybe two, simply loafing about in the sun, taking it easy. We haven't been able to do that for ages. But the point is, we'll have a car – we're hiring one as from next Tuesday in fact, so we could give you and Becky a lift if you like.' He paused, smiling at Candy's amazement.

'Of course,' he went on, 'we needn't meet up at all during the time we're there. But it strikes me that your parents should feel a lot happier about you going to Swaziland if they know Pam and I will be close at hand. And if we are all travelling together, it might also make it easier to get Becky fixed up with whatever documents she's going to need. I'm still not sure why you think she might run into difficulties, but we needn't go into all that now. The two of you had better come and have lunch or dinner with us fairly soon, and we'll bash it all out then . . . Don't worry,' he added, as he saw Candy was about to say something. 'You can leave that side of things to me. I've had a lot of experience in dealing with bureaucracy, and I still know one or two people who could give me any advice that's necessary.'

Candy leaped to her feet, almost spilling the remains of her coffee, and tried to hug him clumsily across the table.

'You're the greatest guy in the world, you know that,' she said.

Uncle Jack held her at bay, chuckling. 'I haven't finished yet,' he warned. 'There's a condition attached to all this. Besides which, I wouldn't like Dirk to hear you saying that. He looks much bigger than I am, judging from the photo you sent me.'

Candy laughed. 'So what's the condition then?'

'You've got to get your parents to agree to the idea.'

'And if I don't – if they still say no?'

'Well, I used to know a snazzy hotel with a swimming pool up in the mountains in Lesotho. It would be an ideal place for Pam and I to . . .'

'Okay. You've made your point.' Candy pulled a face at him. 'Sneaky. The carrot first, and then the whip.'

'Is it a deal?' Uncle Jack asked placidly.

'I'll try,' Candy sighed. 'Believe me, I certainly don't want to hurt my mom and dad if it can be avoided. But you've no idea how difficult it is to get my dad to change his mind when he's already said no to something. He has this crazy, old-fashioned notion that it's bad for discipline. No matter what, you just can't budge him once he's committed himself one way or the other.'

The corners of Uncle Jack's eyes creased in amusement. 'Reminds me of someone else I know,' he remarked.

Candy was put out. However, she managed to grin. 'I guess Dad and I are a bit alike in some ways,' she conceded reluctantly, and they both laughed.

'Oh well, I suppose I'd better be going,' Candy said even more reluctantly. 'My mom will be starting to panic that I've been run over. I came here straight from school, you see.'

'So I gathered,' Uncle Jack informed her drily. He lifted her school hat off the back of the chair and slapped it on her head, pulling it forward over her eyes so she couldn't see.

But when they reached the front door, he became serious for a moment.

'Tell me something, Candyfloss,' he said. 'How many parents do you know who would allow their sixteen-year-old daughter to go off on the sort of holiday you're planning?'

As she gave him a disgruntled look, he went on, 'I'm only mentioning it because I think it might help to bear it in mind when you talk to your parents. After all, the important thing is to keep your cool, don't you agree?'

For answer, Candy stretched up and kissed him on the cheek. 'Now you tell me something,' she said with a sly smile. 'If I was your daughter, would you let me go?'

Uncle Jack chortled. 'That,' he said, 'is the fifty thousand dollar question, isn't it? I think to be fair, you'd better wait and ask me again when I've actually got a sixteen-year-old daughter of my own.'

186

'Then you do intend . . . I hope you are going to have children?'

'We're working on it,' he assured her.

His puckish expression as he waved her off, kept her grinning most of the way home.

*　*　*

'What on earth could have possessed you?' Candy's mother said. She snipped the thorns off the long-stemmed bud she was holding, and pushed it into the vase with unnecessary force. 'Jack's hardly even been here five minutes. Goodness knows what he must think.'

Candy gingerly disentangled another rose from the bunch lying on the table, and silently passed it to her mother.

'I just don't know what's got into you lately,' her mother went on. 'It's been impossible to get a civil word out of you for days. And then to go rushing off to Jack and bothering him with something that doesn't concern him in the slightest. Not the slightest. I can't understand how you could do something like that . . . Washing our dirty linen in public.'

'Uncle Jack isn't exactly the public, Mum. He's my godfather, and I . . .'

'I don't care what he is . . . All right, so he's your godfather. He also happens to be my brother. That's not the point. The fact is you had no right . . . Dad and I told you that you couldn't go to Swaziland and we gave you our reason. That ought to have been the end of it. To then deliberately go behind our backs and . . .' Candy's mother broke off.

Grabbing the last two roses, she rammed them into the vase. Several others promptly toppled over the side, and a few loosened petals fluttered down on the soggy newspaper covering the table-top. With an exclamation of annoyance, she took out the remaining roses and stormed off to get a different vase.

Candy stared after her. Then, feeling slightly sick, she leaned back against the veranda railings and sank her face

187

in her hands. As soon as she heard her mother coming back, she pulled herself up and tried to smile.

'Mum? . . .'

Her mother walked straight past her to the table. She no longer seemed angry. But when she at last raised her eyes, the expression in them made Candy's heart lurch painfully.

'Oh, Mum . . '

For a long moment, they just gazed at each other unhappily in silence. Finally, Candy said in a small, uneven voice, 'I didn't mean to upset you by going to Uncle Jack. I didn't do it as a *deliberate* act of defiance. Honestly.'

'Then why did you do it?'

'Because . . . Because I . . . Well, for a start, I didn't go to Uncle Jack to get him to try and make you change your mind about letting me go to Swaziland. It just sort of came up in the conversation – you know, the fact that I had been wanting to go, but you thought I was too young. Then he mentioned that he would like to take Aunt Pam there for a week or two, and he suggested that maybe we could all go together and he could keep an eye on me for you. That's how it all happened.'

Candy couldn't quite bring herself to look at her mother while she waited for her to answer. Bending down, she picked up a pink petal lying on the floor at her feet and began rubbing it between her hands.

When it became obvious that her mother wasn't going to say anything, she mumbled, 'I'm sorry, Mum. I didn't realize you'd feel so hurt. I thought . . .'

'Yes, well . . . It can't be helped. It's done now.'

In sudden despair, Candy screwed up the crumpled petal and turning, threw it as hard as she could over the railings into the garden.

Perhaps she ought to forget about the whole idea? Perhaps having a holiday in Swaziland with Becky wasn't really worth all the pain involved in fighting with her parents. She

couldn't bear seeing her mother look like this. And yet . . .
But no, she couldn't even feel sure any longer that she was
right. She couldn't feel sure about anything now. Dropping
into the nearest chair, she tried to ease her nausea by massag-
ing her forehead with the tips of her fingers.

She could smell the scent of the crushed petal on her palms.
And suddenly, she remembered how she had been feeling
on Sunday as she had stood at her open bedroom window,
staring out at the garden. For a few moments, she sat very
still with her eyes closed.

'Have you got a headache?'

Candy took her hands away from her face. 'No,' she said.
'I was just thinking.'

'Oh.' Her mother immediately bent her head and went on
with her flower arranging.

'Mum . . . I can't *not* go to Swaziland. I'm sorry, but I
can't. . . . Please believe me, I'm not trying to be a rebel. I
don't want to defy you and Dad. But I must have this holiday
with Becky. I wish I could make you understand. It's not
only that I want it – it's much, much more important than
that. I *need* it, to help me find out what I really think and feel,
for myself. Can you understand that? . . . It's . . . Oh hell . . .
Look, do you remember that day when Becky came to
borrow money from me, and I talked to you about her
afterwards?'

Her mother stepped back and frowned at the half-filled
vase. She turned it round and studied it again, before saying
frostily, 'Well go on then.'

'I told you, didn't I, what she said? – that I sit here seeing
nothing I don't want to . . . That really shook me, you know.'

There was no response.

Candy clasped her hands in her lap to steady them and
continued, 'But that's not all there is to it. I've been realizing
a lot of things lately. Like how conditioned I am by my own
immediate environment. Boy . . .' She grinned faintly. 'That's

the biggest shock of all, that is – when you start to discover how much of what you think and feel and say is simply what you've been taught to think and feel and say. That's why I've got to get away. I've got to get out of all this for a bit. I'm feeling so stifled, so . . . Oh, I don't know.' She jumped up and went to stand on the edge of the steps leading down into the garden.

'Do you realize,' she said over her shoulder, 'that I've known Becky for nearly a year now? Nearly one whole year. Maybe that's not such a long time. But it *feels* like a long time – perhaps because so much has happened. God, when I think what I was like before I met her . . .' She paused to reflect bitterly.

Then she swung round to face her mother and went on passionately, 'Becky's become my closest friend, you know – at least as far as feelings are concerned. She means more to me than all my other friends put together. And yet I can't ring her up and go and visit her whenever I feel like it. I can't go and visit her at all, *ever*. That's another reason why this holiday means so much to me. Staying with Becky's relations won't be the same as visiting her own house, but it will be the next best thing. And most important of all, we'll be able to go out together, *do* things, enjoy ourselves. It'll be two weeks of fantastic freedom. I can't tell you how much I'm looking forward to that.'

Her mother put down the secateurs. 'That's all very well,' she said. 'But have you thought, really thought, what it might be like living with people who have a very different culture from your own? You might find it all very uncomfortable – even horrible, once you get there. What then?'

'I'm sure it won't be that bad.' Candy smiled. 'And it won't do me any harm to have to live more basically for a short while. It'll be good for me, and probably quite healthy too. Especially if Becky's relations live in a rural area.'

'I don't know how you can be so certain. Just say you were to become ill. That wouldn't be so funny, would it.'

'No.' Candy hesitated. '. . . But if anything like that happened, I could always get in touch with Uncle Jack. He'd only be a few miles away. That's why I thought that if you knew he was going, you would . . .' She stopped.

Her mother had snatched up the vase and was walking off. Without looking back she disappeared through the french windows into the dining-room. Before Candy could recover and decide what to do, she reappeared and began clearing up the mess on the table. Candy studied her face despondently.

After a short silence, she braced herself and demanded, 'Aren't you going to say anything, Mum?'

Her mother met her eye coldly. 'What's there to say? You already know how I feel about it all. However . . .' She shrugged. 'As you're obviously still so determined to go, I don't suppose I can stop you.'

They looked at each other across the distance of a few feet. Instinctively, Candy took a step forward.

'I do love you, you know,' she said hoarsely, and she put both her arms round her mother.

'Mhhmm? . . . I wonder.' But her mother let herself be held briefly. 'Will you please let me get on with my work now,' she grumbled. 'I've got a lot to do this afternoon.'

Candy followed her into the dining-room. 'Mum? . . . I'm sorry to be a nuisance . . . But what about Dad?'

'What about him?'

'Will you talk to him? You know what he's like. I don't want to have a row with him. It would be much better if you explained it all to him than if I tried. Please . . .'

'Oh, all right,' her mother said grudgingly. 'I'll have a word with him. I shouldn't expect he'll be too delighted about it. In fact, he's bound to be absolutely furious. Not that you can blame him.' She gave Candy a reproachful look, and started to walk on.

'He won't use physical force to stop me going though, will he?' Candy made herself ask.

'I don't know . . . I don't suppose he'd go that far,' her mother said. She went into the passage, closing the door firmly behind her.

Candy trailed back to the veranda. She flopped down on the settee and covered her face with her hands. She had won, but she felt too emotionally ravaged to have any sense of triumph.

10

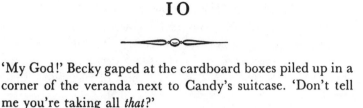

'My God!' Becky gaped at the cardboard boxes piled up in a corner of the veranda next to Candy's suitcase. 'Don't tell me you're taking all *that*?'

Before Candy could answer, Becky had lifted the lid of the top box and was peeping inside.

'Food!... There's tins of meat here for Africa.' She turned round and looked at Candy with her eyebrows raised.

'It wasn't my idea,' Candy explained apologetically. 'My mother insisted that it wasn't fair to expect your relations to feed two extra mouths for two weeks without contributing something. But if you think they will be offended, we can always dump the food somewhere.'

'Don't be crazy.' Becky pulled off her satchel and dropped it on the floor beside the rest of her belongings – two bulging plastic bags. 'She's okay, your mother,' she added, grinning. 'We must remember to get her a present in Swaziland . . . Hey! What's that round your neck?'

'What? . . . Oh this. It's a tiger's eye.' Candy tried to sound nonchalant, but she gave herself away by blushing.

'From the Giraffe, is it?'

'Yes,' Candy admitted. 'He gave it to me last night.'

'Let me see.' Becky brushed Candy's fingers aside and frowned closely at the pendant. 'Mhhmm! . . Nice.'

'It is,' Candy said, and she felt a sudden sharp pang as she remembered the unexpected poignancy of her parting from Dirk in the shadowy darkness outside the front door.

Becky moved back a little and contemplated her with an expression of cynical amusement.

'I suppose you're sorry now that you're going,' she said.

'Of course not. Don't be ridiculous.' Candy hastily pushed

the pendant out of sight beneath her blouse. 'I've been looking forward to this holiday for weeks.'

'Well, I hope you won't be disappointed, that's all.'

'Disappointed? Why should I be disappointed?'

'It's not going to be wildly exciting, you know. My relations don't have a car – just an ox cart.' Becky grinned briefly. '. . . So you won't see very much of Swaziland, that's for sure.'

'I know, I *know*. But I'm not going to Swaziland to find out more about the country – I'm going to find out more about myself.'

For a few moments, Becky was silent, staring at her. Then she nodded thoughtfully, and put her arm round Candy's shoulder.

'Do you remember the very first time we met – in the park, when we drank a toast to our friendship?'

'In Coca-Cola. Yes, I remember,' Candy said, wondering what was coming.

'If we'd only known what we were letting ourselves in for, hey?'

Candy smiled. 'We should have had more sense.'

'That's for sure.' And they both laughed.

'How about another toast now – in coffee?' Candy suggested. 'Actually, I meant to ask you if you've had breakfast?'

'Hours ago.'

'Well, if you're hungry, there are some sandwiches in that plastic container on the table. My mother made them in case we wanted a snack on the journey. I'll go and put the kettle on – won't be a tick.'

As she dashed into the kitchen, Candy almost collided with her mother who was carrying a loaded breakfast tray.

'Careful! . . . What's the rush?' her mother said. 'Surely Jack and Pam can't be here already. Heavens, I haven't even brushed my hair yet.'

'It's all right,' Candy assured her. 'Uncle Jack said half

past and he's never early. There's loads of time. I'm going to make Becky and myself some coffee.'

'Oh. I didn't know Becky had arrived. Where is she?' Involuntarily, her mother's eyes flickered towards Tom who was standing at the stove, stirring his mealie-meal porridge.

'It's all right, Mum,' Candy said again, trying not to sound irritable. 'She's on the veranda.'

Her mother went slightly red. 'Well . . . I'll come and say hallo in a minute . . . Drat! There's some tea in this saucer. Here, hold the tray, will you dear. I'd better mop it up. Dad can't stand a messy saucer.'

Candy's heart sank at the mention of her father. But she remained silent until her mother had taken the tray back. Then she asked, 'He's not ill, is he?'

'No, he's just having a lie-in this morning.'

Their eyes met. They both knew very well that Candy's father never stayed in bed late on a Saturday. At the week-ends, he was always the first member of the family to be up and about.

'He's keeping . . .', Candy had to clear her throat, '. . . out of the way. Is that it?'

Her mother shot a glance at Tom and then jerked her head to indicate Candy was to follow her.

They stopped a little way up the passage and looked at each other. Candy forced herself to smile.

'It's okay,' she said. 'You don't have to say anything.' The answer she dreaded was all too plainly visible on her mother's face. 'I didn't really expect him to want to say goodbye to me.'

She turned on her heel and went back down the passage.

'I've put the kettle on for you, Miss Cand,' Tom called from the scullery.

'Thanks, Tom.' She kept her head down, hiding her face from him while she got the coffee things ready.

'Miss Cand?'

Candy took a firm hold on herself. 'Yes, Tom?'

'Can you bring me a bottle of sea water from Swaziland for my stomach?'

'I'm afraid not. There isn't any sea in Swaziland. Anyway, you shouldn't drink sea water. It'll rot your insides.'

He gave her an amused look. 'Don't you know, it's very, very, very good *muthi*.* Curranteed. Next time I'll give you some. Then you'll see.'

'Urggh! No, you won't.' But she was laughing now. Never mind his sea water, she thought. He was a 'curranteed' *muthi* himself, if he only knew it.

'Perhaps there's something else I could bring you from Swaziland instead?' she asked after a moment.

'Like what, Miss Cand?'

'I don't know.' She stretched past him for the kettle. 'Anything you want. You tell me.'

When he didn't answer, she glanced at him through the steam. He was staring across the room.

Candy looked round. Becky was standing in the doorway, smiling uncertainly at them both.

'Uh . . . Hallo,' Candy stammered. 'Uh . . . Becky, this is . . . Tom . . . Mr . . . uh . . .'

'Hallo,' Becky said quickly to Tom.

'Hallo.' He gave her an almost imperceptible nod. Then he turned abruptly and went into the scullery.

Becky grinned at Candy. 'I came to see if I could carry something.' If she was embarrassed, it didn't show in her voice or her face.

Candy's own face felt as if it was on fire. 'Oh, yes,' she said. 'The sugar. It's over there. I'll just finish pouring and then we . . .'

But Becky had already disappeared quietly, taking the sugar with her.

Tom was making a lot of noise at the sink. Candy studied

* *medicine*

196

his back wretchedly for nearly a minute before she made up her mind and crossed the room.

'Tom? . . .'

'Yes?' His voice sounded gruffer than usual and he didn't look up.

Candy hesitated. 'Tom, do you know who that girl is?'

He shook his head and bent down to pick up a fork that had fallen on the floor.

'She's the friend I'm going to Swaziland with.'

Tom said nothing while he scoured out the sink and dried his hands. Then he asked in a carefully neutral tone, 'Is she the one who's coming every Sunday? Your Zulu teacher?'

'She is, yes.' After a long pause, Candy added hesitantly, 'Do you mind?'

'Mind?' He glanced at her for an instant. 'What you mean, Miss Cand?'

Candy blushed. She didn't want to have to go into details. The subject was too sensitive, and she was still smarting from her humiliating awkwardness over the introductions.

'Well, are you upset?' she asked finally.

'No. Why you think that?' He gave her a grin as if to prove there was nothing wrong with him. 'I'm plenty too much happy you going away. Now I don't have to dust your books for two weeks.'

Candy smiled, thankful that there was no need to pursue the subject further. In a sudden rush of emotion, she put her hands on his shoulders.

'You look after yourself while I'm away, you hear?' she told him.

'I will. You too, Miss Cand.'

'Tom, I – ' and then she caught her breath sharply. She dropped her hands with an embarrassed laugh, and went back to the table to finish making the coffee.

As she was about to leave the room, she stopped and looked at him over her shoulder. He had his head down, peering short-sightedly into an enamel bowl. His hair had been shaved recently, and the bald shape of his skull, showing the small folds of wrinkles across the back of his neck, made him seem suddenly very vulnerable.

'Tom . . . don't you lose any more teeth while I'm gone, will you?'

'*More* teeth, Miss Cand? I've got no more teeth already. They're all finished now. Maybe you better bring me some new ones from Swaziland.'

'I'll try,' Candy promised. 'I'll try very, very, very hard.' And she went away, comforted by his cheerful chuckle which followed her as far as the hall.

She found Becky sitting alone on the veranda, reading a magazine and eating a sandwich.

'Sorry I was so long,' Candy mumbled. 'Here's your coffee.'

Becky gave her a sideways glance. 'Thank you, Miss Cand,' she said coyly.

'That's not funny,' Candy snapped. She knew she was over-reacting, but she couldn't take being teased about Tom – not in her present mood. 'It isn't like that with Tom and me,' she went on indignantly. 'I've asked him not to call me Miss. But I realize now that he doesn't use it as a term of respect. It's a sort of endearment. When he's cross with me, he simply calls me Candy. That's why I know he . . .'

'Okay, okay. I'm sorry. I was only teasing. It's the truth. I didn't mean to make you angry.'

Candy calmed down at the penitent look on Becky's face. '*I'm* sorry,' she muttered. 'I guess I'm a bit jumpy this morning.'

'That's okay. It's my fault. My feet are too big sometimes.'

They shared a grin, but more guardedly than usual, and Candy was relieved to see Uncle Jack's hired Toyota turn in at the gateway just then.

'They're early,' she said. 'Better drink up fast.' She gulped her own coffee, and ran to the door to give her mother a shout.

The next few minutes were a confusion of noise and excitement with everybody talking at once. After the initial greetings were over, Candy left her mother chatting to Uncle Jack and Aunt Pam at the car, and followed Becky on to the veranda to gather up their luggage.

'Boxes first, I suppose,' Becky said, bending down to pick one up.

Candy didn't answer. She was looking at Colin, who had come out of the house and was looking past her at Becky. He stood still for a second or two indecisively, watching Becky struggle to lift the box. Then he seemed to make up his mind suddenly, and strode towards her.

'I'd better take that,' he said. 'It's too heavy for you.'

Becky turned round and grinned at him. 'Why thank you,' she said. 'It is very heavy,' and she stepped aside.

As soon as he had gone, Becky pulled a face at Candy. 'Do you think he'll be asking me out next?' she whispered.

'I'm sure he'd like to,' Candy spluttered. She realized Becky must have seen through Colin from the very beginning.

'He's okay, really,' Becky went on. 'He shall overcome. His heart's in the right place . . . No, I mean that.'

'Yes,' Candy said, and she glanced fondly after Colin's retreating back.

'If only,' she thought, 'Dad would come out now.' But she knew that was asking too much. Life never gave you what you wanted without making you pay for it in some way. 'I have no regrets,' she told herself staunchly. 'I have to follow my own convictions.'

Nevertheless, when all the goodbyes had been said and the others had already climbed into the car, Candy felt a need to hang back and give her mother a last hug.

'Thanks Mum. For everything,' she said softly. Then she

found herself adding, 'Perhaps . . . Would you say goodbye to Dad for me?'

Her mother nodded and squeezed her more tightly before releasing her.

'Now are you sure you haven't forgotten anything, dear?' she said when Candy had got into the car. 'Your toothbrush? . . . Towel? . . . And your hat? Did you pack your hat? I don't want you getting sunstroke.'

'You sound just like my mother,' Becky told her, laughing.

'I do?' Candy's mother looked surprised. But she recovered quickly and gave a little giggle. 'Well, anyway, have a nice time, the pair of you. And remember to write, won't you? Even if it's only a postcard. Otherwise I'll be worried if I don't hear anything.'

'We'll write to you,' Becky promised. '*Sala kahle.*'

'Oh yes . . . *Sally kahle.*' Candy's mother giggled again. 'No. That's not right, is it. What am I supposed to say, dear? . . . *Hamby kahle.* Yes. *Hamby kahle.*'

'Not *Hamby*, Mum. It's *Hamba kahle.*'

Colin snorted loudly from the veranda. '*Hamby kahle* indeed.' He shook his head at his mother, and turned to go into the house. ''Bye,' he called back vaguely as an after-thought. 'Have a good time.'

Uncle Jack put the car in gear and it started to move forward slowly. 'Don't worry, Sue,' he said through the window at the last moment. 'We'll keep an eye on these young scamps for you.'

Candy dumped her bag at her feet, and swung round to wave as the car picked up speed down the drive. A second figure had joined her mother at the bottom of the steps. It wasn't Colin. It was . . .

'Stop!' Candy cried.

Uncle Jack jammed on the brakes. Before the car had come to a complete standstill, Candy was out and running back towards the house. She didn't have time to think about what she was doing, or what she would say to her father when she reached him. She only knew it was desperately important to her to have his blessing on this undertaking. Her whole future relationship with him seemed to be at stake on this one issue.

She pulled up, panting, in front of him.

'Forgotten something, have you?'

Candy flinched at his forbidding tone. 'No, Dad.'

He eyed her coldly in silence.

'I've come to say goodbye.'

'I see.'

It took Candy's last reserve of courage to lean forward and kiss him on the chin.

''Bye Dad,' she said, and somehow she succeeded in smiling into his eyes.

He didn't respond immediately. But Candy thought she saw a slight twitch deepen the creases in his cheeks.

'Hmm! You definitely must take after your mother,' he remarked dourly.

'And exactly what is that supposed to mean?' Candy's mother demanded.

'Never mind.' This time, the twitch was unmistakable. 'You don't give up, do you?' he said to Candy.

Candy's smile widened. She had detected a faint note of respect in his voice, and she felt a sudden warmth spreading through her.

'Dad . . .'

'Run along then,' he interrupted her gruffly. 'Don't keep them waiting.' He almost allowed himself to smile as he added, 'Enjoy yourself. And see that you behave.'

'Yes. 'Bye. Take care, both of you.'

Candy ran back to the car on winged feet. She leaped in beside Becky, and slammed the door.

'Sorry,' she gulped.

Uncle Jack winked at her in the rear view mirror. He let

off the handbrake, and the car shot forward through the gate and down the road.

'Well, we're on our way,' Aunt Pam commented happily, settling herself more comfortably in her seat.

'Yes,' Candy agreed silently. Right then, she could believe that they all really were. But she was afraid to be too optimistic. They had only barely taken a first step. There was a long, long way to go yet, and she had a feeling that time was running out. All the same, she told herself, simply to have started was something; at least there was hope in that.

'Are you okay?'

Becky's quiet question snapped Candy out of her reverie. She sat back and smiled.

'*Yebo*,' she said.

'You sure?'

'Absolutely. But I still can't quite believe that we're actually going on holiday together.'

Becky pretended to give the matter careful thought. Finally she said, with the merest shadow of a grin, 'I can tell you. It's the truth.'